Sarah Bastard's
Notebook

Sarah Bastard's Notebook

Marian Engel

INSOMNIAC PRESS

Series edited by Richard Almonte
Interior design by Mike O'Connor

Library and Archives Canada Cataloguing in Publication

Engel, Marian, 1933-1985.
[No clouds of glory]
    Sarah Bastard's notebook / Marian Engel.

(Insomniac library)
First published: Don Mills, Ont., Longmans Canada, 1968 under
    title: No clouds of glory.
ISBN 1-897178-12-3

    I. Title. II. Series.

PS8559.N5N6 2006   C813'.54   C2005-907616-X

The publisher gratefully acknowledges the support of the Canada
Council, the Ontario Arts Council and the Department of
Canadian Heritage through the Book Publishing Industry
Development Program.

Printed and bound in Canada

Insomniac Press
192 Spadina Avenue, Suite 403,
Toronto, Ontario, Canada, M5T 2C2

à Bonheur-la-Chance

I

I have had, now, time to recover; a smooth week in the womb. Everything rained, and turned green, pouring past the window. A sopping, tropical heat has yanked the morning glories up against the window; they are obscene, like dolls whose hair screws up with a key.

I tried to go home. The wreck of my Oedipus complex asked for a saccharine library book, and I fled.

The old men crawl out of their lairs, earthworms after the rain. Their hostel is closed, they hang around the booze cans shouting for Bill, Phil, Pete, the love of Mike, and Fucking Christ. In the park, they tell what Swedenborg and Jesus did for them. Toronto.

Joe didn't belong to me. We were borrowers of each other, in need of a laugh or a poke, or a proof-reading; come to Sarah for soup. I couldn't see what the arrangement lacked, it kept these crooked walls from licking me, he had to live somewhere. Unhealthy, Ma said, and no doubt, but it seemed to me function-al. Pity he's gone, my last prop. I'll have to suture that scar before I bleed.

Of a sudden, seven ducks... everything goes up in smoke. Job, family, *erotiko* and *agapo*, beginning of a reputation. Here I stand, naked, if anyone had eyes to see, waiting for the evaluator; feeling, for that, almost nothing. Self-pity, perhaps, as if the doctor had commanded a salt-free diet. Simple, empty, in spite of myself nourished on hope: waiting for the new era to begin. Finally satisfied to be alone? Finally free?

But if it had gone on, if everything had stayed the same? Apocalypse.

I should begin at the beginning if there were one, but all beginnings belong inside people, and my reading of my own entrails has been unscientific.

I keep having to remind myself that I shall not improve. Unchristian, but true. You always stay what you are. Fortunately, you do not always have to stay where you are.

So what does matter? Whose new flag (red on a Kotex, *garni*)? Whose funeral? Whose thwarted career, birth, marriage?

Life and death; these from the inside, if communicated.

Oh, I am very much of my age and stage. Communicate is one of my words, and I expect people to live up to it. Sarah Porlock, Bastard and Fool.

Father's death mattered, but they tried to take it away from him. Fancy waking up dead, unwarned, having missed it. I should wait for my death (and confess I am impatient, and I have sometimes played with suicide) as if it were a frightful birthday. Is it today? They said in the hospital, "Don't tell him, let him hope." Unhappy, he was, and the Christless Protestants, not allowing him to prepare. He died unshriven, though one doubts that he had any sins, aside from a dislike of the Chinese. He held my hand in his great one that was not made for the life of a civil servant (is captivity carcinogenic?). "What do they say?"

"What do you want them to say?"

"I want to live."

"Go on, then, live." Nerve kept his old aunties alive to their nineties. And he was blue, and only sixty-three. Pouchy, shrunken, skin like onion paper. "Are you afraid?"

"I don't know, Sarah, I don't know."

"Live by what you taught me. Brave and respectful, you can't lose." I am a liar, again and again; respectful you lose, we had learned that together, I hoped. You have to be rude in this great friendly dog-fight. Respect is no longer a learning stage. If death doesn't, why should life?

I told him, "You have only to respect God. Everyone else is human." He looked disapproving, but proud. You could see his drowning man's life on his inner screen: irrepressible country boy begets soldier begets hero begets martyr, begets minor civil servant, begets Steward of Church, begets old man in hospital. My good years, these last twelve since leaving home and school, were his horror. Canadian Tommy marches off to feed cannon, irreverent Christian soldier; is told he's one of a subject people, slotted into a trench until he beats the racket, goes up in a rat-tat-tat batwinged flying machine: goggles, joy sticks (whose joy?), fur boots, and little Winnie Churchill. A medal or two, no parachutes. Crutches, slings, nurses with husbands in Hyderabad. That too could be poetry, or verse at least, but soon enough he's home down the St. Lawrence, and no job but limping to a secretarial college, no pension for a short leg. A boring little clerk-ship his father finally buys him. His goodwife, my mother. Then, us, four daughters. The Depression, a series of provincial offices in provincial towns; cancer before retirement. Will my life become the kaleido-scope his was, of forms and fears?

I am not surprised that his generation during the Depression turned to God. I am only angry that they tried to take away his death.

Perhaps in those antipathetic hospitals, they are ashamed not to be able to sterilize the unknown. No, it is that they are afraid to admit that there is an unsterilizable unseen. Here's your hypo, old man, and don't tell me the angels of God come flying through ethylene compounds of dreamless nylon sleep. You have to wait up for the angels, Pa, don't miss them, now. If you drug away the pain always, there won't be any release.

Doctor calls me an unfeeling fool. Doesn't believe in Taylor, Jeremy.

"He's a grown man, my father."

"You want to make him suffer."

"I want him to know where he is. A religious man deserves it."

I was overruled. A sort of euthanasia prevailed. For him, at any rate, the joys of consciousness had died long ago. After the civil service set in he was a good, kind, frightened example of his unlucky genera-tion: half killed for dead England, the rest parboiled to the memory of Victoria, sent victorious in this coun-try long after everywhere else. Respect. Do not enjoy, or be aware. Advance carefully to Go, collect $200, and be grateful for the rest of your life.

Not the first death in the history of the world. Only in my world.

I was on my way to the funeral home when the weather changed. Got off the streetcar by a Specialty Shoppe to replace my elastic casings with a garter belt, stave off dying myself, and was out in the street again before I remembered, no pants. It didn't seem right, going to the funeral home without pants, so I went back in; and all the store had was six bucks' worth of white eyelet, with thick frills, for under tennis skirts or over outsize babies. They made great ridges under my skirt, and all I could think of when I looked at his waxy, manicured self was, which would be less respectful, none, or this humiliation? So this was why they invented the soul, to take your mind off your underwear. But I got to the soul too late to show the right feelings; the circles of red eyes had found me out. My sisters and my mother had seen more death than I had, they knew I was thinking of something else. I wanted to argue, convert them to another reality. Instead, I hurried away.

We should have had a wake. Ah, if they could wail, stink, confess, weep wealthily! But there was to be four days of tea drinking, and this was only the first one.

My office smelled by association of hypodermics, embalming fluid, death, drudgery. Not so many women get to say "my office," but the pleasure of that gone, I had to get on with the bursting of my life.

Except insofar as it began when I was born, the bursting, the burgeoning of round, ribbed, pod-Sarah into milkweed floss—useless, directionless—began with an interview for the *Toronto Star*.

You see, I have—had until recently—a position to keep up. I am a lady Ph.D. One of an increasing multitude, but in my own point in time and space, a rare enough bird, the only one the paper felt like rooting out that year, the only one at my college under fifty, and their series was on "Young Canadians." And two weeks ago, I hadn't yet turned thirty.

The mental marbles of my corniced shelves are formidable—Hopkins, Gide, Apollinaire, Sartre, and Beckett, Joyce, Eliot, Hemingway, and Gertrude. Footsteps worth studying. But those of us who operate from bastard territory, disinherited countries and traditions, long always for our nonexistent mothers. For this reason, I deviled five years—six? when did I start? how many?—in the literature of Australians and Canadians, hoping to be the one to track her down. In the nineteenth century there were unashamed Colonials. In the twentieth a few geniuses, and a host of Sarahs looking for themselves; too late finding their modes and models. First books appear, followed by silence, or by forays into unconvincing commercialism. Or "satire," the holding of pain at arm's length instead of loving it; or this nostalgia, the one tradition Canadians follow well.

Australians are just about as dull.

"Jump into Amcan," one of our less deadly writers had a character advised, "there's the field for you . . ." Austcan is even emptier, sir, and leads more surely to the Slough of Despond. I've published, sir; the competition isn't tough, though there are better people than I in the field. I'm an authority. I've read more dull books than anyone else you know. I've done honest work, sir. I'm a historian of despair.

Honest? Honest work?

Listen, I'm as big a liar and a cheat as anyone else. Someone tells me, "Sair, you're the only person I know who's *trying.*" I listen spellbound to my virtues, forgetting the uselessness of documenting lost hopes. It's a field for a good bibliographer, and a field, also, for optimists—there will be something there one day. But for Sarah? The opportunist opportuned. Jump into Austcan, lady, in five years you'll have it—almost—to yourself.

And then they'll send somebody around from the newspapers and you'll be famous, just the way you always wanted to be.

So, that Saturday, I went to see my father in the funeral home, and then I read my mail. Two letters, and a marked newspaper.

Quick, Sarah, talk about something else.

Four daughters, my father has, a spongy collection. We adhere, with gaps.

Rosemary is eldest, has a Porlock sense of propriety, a pretty face, and a hatchet will that storms out from behind her public, charming façade. Like Toronto, she rejects the subconscious; was widowed at twenty-two, and is tough. Her second husband is rich, and they are raising six kids, her first son Mark, and five of their own, a conscientiously enriched generation. Never mind, she'll be a grandmother one day.

Then Peg, who is quiet, who married Eldon, who is not. She is a botanical artist, and he lectures, as I did, long ago, two weeks ago, at St. Ardath's College.

Then Leah, then me. Night and day, all the clichés. She's ten months older and began with the inestimable advantage of having her name changed from Leda, when Mother read about the swan.

A woman on our street had ten children and died satisfied, they all married Protestants. Leah's husband is Catholic, and all mine were borrowed—but returned.

Two letters and a newspaper, after the private view. I postpone opening them, I still have work. I'm filling in final marks on IBM cards with intentions to staple or bend. A musty afternoon, but I've never been able to throw a letter out unread.

Two letters.

I don't mind scenes, I mind silence, they know that, but neither—sometimes I say, greedily, both—is the sort to come and tell me. "Dear Sarah, these last two years have been a salvation, and I am grateful, and would like them to go on. However, I was told yesterday that I could begin now to make a new home for Ruth..."

Joe is packing, then.

"Dear Sarah, I have decided not to risk a confrontation, and will not come to your father's funeral. I am sure that to your mother, New York is very far away, and I have written to say that business will not permit..."

Sandro is unpacking, now. Who's he got in New York?

Neither. Both. None.

Well, I've no desire for marriage. I'm not going to settle for company, status, the end of sick loneliness. Joe was my friend, I met him in my freshman year, we were buddies, companions, lovers—everything, at one time or another. Lately, my lodger; we were living rather more than openly together, hoping to heal despair. We loved in other directions, but I've caught us both thinking—maybe she won't ever come back, and we can stay this way. My Sandro not being mine, and Joe's wife Ruth, mad.

Living with women disgusts me, and an empty flat is empty. Cats are obvious. I'm not so much a rover I can take sex where I find it, I still count my men on my fingers. We were wrong for each other, we said, Joe and I, but to be used to fend off darkness is to have a place in the world. "Who prop, thou ask'st, in these bad days, my mind?" He much, the young man, Joe.

As I grow older, and today I am incredibly old, tortoise-necked, scaly-headed, dyed henna and scurfy and drawn, as I grow older by leaps that others avoid, and look younger because of my fatuous nose and filled cheeks, I am increasingly fascinated by relationships and their stages. I have become a voyeur of other people's couplings, watching the dark call to the fair, the fat to the lean, the platitudes of wedding photographs develop themselves. And the subtler marriages we go on seeking all our lives, as we develop our identities, or cease to. And the mad matings as friends, on the presumption that sex is knowledge (sex is rest), screw their own reflections or the obverse of their ideas of themselves; or fag after their own hopes. These I watch, catching them out in their oversimplifications, their thinking that the fault with life is a simple dichotomy, that if opposites and equals are joined, a solution will be evident, easy, and practical; trying to mend their own fissures by resort to easy dialectic; thinking themselves halved when they are atomized. I go on watching, and in myself melting and re-forming day after day; like everyone else, never twice the same person, always the same, and something between. It is not good to be born a watcher; it has robbed me of too much hope.

My sister Leah appeared to be a watcher too, but in the end, I found her interests were less timidly academic than mine. She watched to see what the others did, to do the opposite, or to make use of them, or to improve her secret history of herself. People might have taken us for twins, we were that close in age; they at least forced the dialectic on us: beauty/truth, light/dark, introvert/extrovert, down to the blue pajamas and the pink. And if Snow White was feckless and lovely, Rose Red must be earnest and fat. We went to St. Ardath's in the same year; she fell quickly by the wayside into the role of the Carnival Queen. I was marked at once for Academia, and began meeting Joe inside the door of the Roxy Cinema once a week for intellectual films.

Given provincial standards, we were all, to our parents, a trial. Rosemary, tutored in Latin, married too young; Peg had TB, was exiled to the unmentionable San. After St. A's, Leah sulked through secretarial school, and, in her disturbing way, began working only as long as she wanted to, a month here, a month there, and faithfulness is the core of our moral code. Met every rebuff with silence, fazed my strong mother like some little wild witch, had a life of her own while none of the rest of us dared (we did give a damn what our parents thought, and their neighbors) and acted on the presumption they'd not dare to throw her out. She was right. Not a born watcher, then, but a skeptic.

I always believed what my mother said. Was I lazy? Still in the poison ivy enjoying the fumble at the brassière hooks when my friends were bedding, marrying, breeding; stupid enough to believe what the elders said about men, holding fast to Sunday School morality because it was work to devise another one. I was burying the teen-agers' contraceptives in the sand when neat cat Leah found another way out.

For one last summer we are together—twenty-one, twenty-two, twenty-five, twenty-seven. At the cottage, all of us, Mother beginning to look pinched, unconvinced at last by the virtues of family unity. Leah has quit her job, Peg works wherever she is, Rosemary lives at home, and I play the young genius on scholarship, typing into the night.

Leah lies naked in the shallow water, staring at the sky. Here, at the sandy edge, it is four inches deep, warm as broth. Reeds like chives, and minnows. Rosemary ties a cotton sunhat on her boy, her treasure, and takes out knitting. Peg, with a saving sigh, draws in the veins of the cinquefoil. I cry out "What's the point?"

This is not one day, but the consummation of our summer days. It is written on the scroll of our summer life that Leah soaks and stares, Peg works, Rosemary domesticates, I stand on the verandah looking for the white charger that will save me from scholarship. "If," says a voice inside me, "you are expecting a personal letter from God explaining your particular point, you are indeed to be disappointed." I refuse to accept my situation until that personal letter arrives. Scholarship is what, in a limited way, I am good at, and what I have no patience for. I pray that someone will find me out and fail me, save me from the chauvinistic displeasure of Comparative Australian and Canadian Literature. Meanwhile, I go east and west, back into time and to the end of it, seeking a more special fate.

Leah has found her karma: big, blossoming nothing. Since Ma banned bikinis she has worn nothing. She sunbathes two centimeters under the water so as not to tan her tits. (She has tits, I have boobs, that forever is the difference between us.) She lies there all day, during the week, until we want to scream at her "Focus!" Sometimes Mother sends one of us to warn of the approach of the iceman, just to break the monotony. If she did not also spend hours at Dostoevski, we'd be sure she was a half-wit. One day, I think, a romantic fisherman will discover her and think her a painted Venus. The man-woman ratio in this house will then be one to four, but by now Pa is used to leaking outside.

Rosemary is absorbed in her knitting, and in this brown boy who will never be naked or less than half-orphaned, wholly hers. She makes a good widow. Ate her mate to save her son from the world: better than the wife of the Author of Beltraffio, but more ordinary. She keeps watch over her animated doll; when I am allowed to bathe him I look for the embossed "A Reliable Toy" on his nape.

Peg draws fine, pubic things: veins, hairs on petals, little seeds; a tatooist on paper. She is all nerves and neatness, remote. You can't see her sick shadows from here. What mysteries did she learn besides drawing in her sanitarium?

The beach shines wide and white. We are the last of the lucky ones, with our own stretch of lake, the cottage my great-grandfather's unspoiled and arid homestead, which we have little money to spoil by restoration. A little island sits placid in the lap of our bay. Father is away until the weekend.

Rosemary breaks a double-yolked egg for Mark's lunch. Ma would like to do it, but Mark is Rosemary's toy. Leah is here, but not here; she has rescued her bathing suit from under a stone and stroked out to the island. I cannot decide whether Australian writers are less repellent than Canadian, everybody is genteel, I like my sex vicarious and there's none.

In our olden days this was paradise. Drive up on the first of July, each with six library books, excited, stopping for me to be sick, get take-away sundaes at the Owen Sound dairy, with peach-and-maraschino jam for sauce. First, leagues of summer greenery, white farms, and cows; then ruined, raddled dry farmsteads; national excitement at the first outcrops of rock; lilacs, grey fences of stumps: it is *north*. On the peninsula there are swamps where we hope for water moccasins among the yellow lilies; then sand dunes, Mrs. Weeder's farm, five cents for the first sight of the lake, the dirt-covered corduroy road to our place.

We share the bay with the Weeders, so there are cow pies in the sand; they have fishing boats and an icehouse. Wid Weeder pays a nickel for a dozen baby frogs and is something called a Reeve; his mother is a witch. Pa and Rosemary get out the boat and go fishing, first day, far out where the bass and pickerel are, to stock the live box. The creek bed is full of watercress and little perch which we are not allowed to catch and keep, as Father respects the law.

But we get older and there are whole summers when we stay away, I with my passion for institutions going to camp, Peg in her San, the others, who remembers? Up here, we retain old habits, Rosie is Wid Weeder's friend and Leah heads for the island, her territory because she learned to swim first. I leave her there, and stick to the shore and the woods, paradises of old sawlogs, whippoorwills' nests, cans of toads. There was an ants' nest under a board we were allowed to turn up once a day, to see the mothers hurry their Rice Krispies away. We could all four of us be queens up there, but I think some of us wanted to be kings. It is the lyric north my countrymen write books about; it has a strong seduction, and is meaningless.

Oh, sometimes we behave like ordinary people, play rummy, talk at night by the Coleman lantern while the bobby pins flack in and out of their plastic box. "Sarah," Leah whispers, "have you made love yet, to a man?"

"Of course not." I am cross, she has interrupted the thought with the subject.

"Mother thinks I have."

"She would." Mother thinks pamphlets labeled

"Playing with Fire" are tact.

"What are you going to do when you finish your M.A., read more books?"

"You read as much as I do."

"You read for a living."

One way of thinking about it. I walked three miles for what I'm reading now, though, and it's not stuff you get paid to inspect unless you're the censor. I want her to shut up. She has a secret triumphant look on her face, we know what she thinks of reading.

"Do you want to get married?"

"Sure." She has hair like pull taffy and I hate the way she coils it. She'll be loved all right for her yellow hair—and I?

"I think I'll get married."

"Oh, I bet you will. Just let me know when and I'll come throw stones at the church." The book I was reading wouldn't impress a farm boy of seventeen, but my knees were rising and I wanted to be alone and pant.

"Jealous? Well I won't be around much longer."

"Don't make it sound like a threat."

She'd gone away a couple of times before, and Mum and Rosemary had run with grappling hooks to bring her back, or make her stay stuck in the Anglican hostel in Toronto; but now she was of age. I figured I wouldn't mind if she were gone, just gone. I hated being half of "us" and "them." If we had been twins, there might have been some compensating communion; but we existed only to be thrown at each other. As it sometimes happens in families, she was called "demanding" because she demanded to be left alone; they went streaming past me after her, and called me "self-sufficient."

I can't be remote, I suffer from agoraphobia. Yes, Mother, no Mother, yes Rosie, no Peg; I hate, I love, anything but silence. Just for attention, I take the blame for Leah, until they find me a clownish masochist. But if I fake illness, hers is real; I earn praise, but their eyes are on her naughtiness: get the hell out, Leah, let me live.

She did.

A ship, an isle, a sickle moon: all the claptrap. She swam to the island and was not there at sunset. On the dresser in our room she left a note: "I have gone away to get married, I am not coming back. Don't worry, Leah."

We had seen the boat, dredging or diving, exploring, perhaps, the minor shipwrecks in the outer islands, far out, for days, but we were not scientifically inclined. Rosie drove over to ask Wid Weeder what the men had been about, came back screaming "Italians." That her son should be related to such a woman as Leah.

Mother wept a little, I wondered if with relief. I was satisfied that she was gone.

I said to a man in the mountains, once, when we were building structures of enjoyment in the brisk and footloose air, that those of us who grow up in romantic scenery continue subject to its dangerous charm. We carpeted our afternoon with Swedes, Norwegians, Australians, Americans, Canadians, Russians: inheri-

tors of grandeur and space, forever because of it sentimental. The poetry of the land drives us away from living; we try instead to construct epics; early, our diseased consciousness seeks the remote and exotic, there
are always the mountains on the horizon, blinding us to
extant reality, which we think of as worms. We cannot
describe our surroundings without encrusting them
with sugar; we speak another generation's hyperbole
and deny there is evil in the happy land.

Anne of Green Gables wanted to be sweet, good,
and true, and I was impressed. When we were good at
home, we could drink our milk from bowls like Heidi.
There were also the impulses from the vernal wood:
we got on that wavelength early and some of us never
got off. Mother and Rosie still think symbolism and
psychoanalysis are dirty, and I know I would like to.
Give me the old, fictional virtues that belong to the
land of spruce and pine and I'll trade myself in on a
good, sweet, true piece of womanhood that has nothing to do with the case.

Where we lived in the winter was a rickety house,
peeled stucco at the back. There was the Housing
Shortage, so the parents slept in the dining room,
Leah and I in the room with the draught, and Rosie in
the sunroom. Old pussy of a landlady with pince-nez
lived upstairs, but refused to concede her piano to our
need for *Lebensraum*, so that we were the only people
in town with two, and the Ladies' Morning Musical
Club marched over our hospitality to trill without
accepting a cup of tea, and formed my politics.
Mother, being good and sweet and true, was patient.
One of the Ladies had red hair and her husband left

her. I was glad. Before that, I had planned to kill her.

On that street, there were Cathlicks on either side of us. The ones on the right must have been, contrary to our belief about Cathlicks, rich, because their pajamas were made out of the same calico as our Sunday summer dresses. They had figure skates and curly hair. Cathlicks were a mystery, a romance. You could speak to them, but not marry them, the priests took your babies away. The girls had long hair, and the nuns used hatpins to keep order in music lessons, and school was mostly prayers.

We did not even then let reality seep through. Society helps those who help themselves. At school there are the Big Girls and the Little Girls, all the same age, but the Big Girls don't tell the Little Girls what they tell each other, and they all seem to have Started, and congregate in corners to tell each other stories that we at the same age are not old enough to hear. Instinct tells who will marry from grade eight.

Father tells us we must make our way in life, with self-discipline and industry. He would try to instill feminine virtues but cannot quite remember what they are, feminine reality (hundreds of pairs of pants on the line) having obscured his vision.

To get caught again in that romance, to tell again the story of everyone's blissful Canuck childhood: little well-fed kings and queens against a landscape. Jesus said we should be like little children, and we are until they throw in St. Paul, and we put joy carefully in mothballs, concentrate on the symbols of maturity, accomplishment reflected in the car, the job, the family, all acquired through institutional approval. We forgo the childish pleasures of decoration, learning, and creating in order to earn, spend, and breed. Our eyes are fixed on distant mountains, we are buying the equipment to get there, a camping trip to the Rockies, every kid knowing how to use an axe and open a can of beans, that's the epitome. We drive fast toward annihilation and where we have not time to create, subscribe. And if I had been asked to join the race, I should have gone as fast as anybody else.

Viz. the article in the newspaper.

Two letters and a newspaper I said I got, on a significant Saturday—the day after my father died—Joe tells me he's leaving, Sandro reneges on the funeral visit. And there is an article on Sarah in the Saturday paper that leaves me without excuse. It is not even one of God's fools that I have been.

What day did the reporter come? Two weeks ago on a Friday, before the carbuncle of death and destruction burst. One of those late spring mornings that start icy, then run a temperature. I wanted to stay home and make love to Joe, and had instead to mark papers. I was wearing a moth-eaten pullover, tights, and a skirt with egg on it. Still half asleep, I flung myself on my papers, sweating in that strange womb my office until I excreted unreality and claustrophobia. Longing for Joe, I had to be satisfied with freshmen on Ruskin, and when the young reporter came I was estranged indeed.

A flat-faced, antipathetical, sneering kind of boy, English accent verging on Sidcup, the good soil of English unwashedness still clinging to his armpits, giving the lie to his rayon Old-Etonian tie; diffident, hostile, not to be taken seriously. "Look here, young man," I said, because he was a bad-dream boy, not a real reporter, "let's piss off for a beer."

And my father in that hospital dying.

Fat, self-pity, my own unwashedness, nicotine, and beer, spawned words. Hated because female, nonconformist, self-important, intellectual, free, fucking, undressed-gorgeous, too good for this place, here. He began to look sick. After a sixth draft I went home to sleep it off. He wrote it, all, all down.

Home is the sailor, home from the sea.

Sarah goes down in history...

No Rodgers and Hart girl this (though I count my fingers as bluely, as ginnily) but a "vigorous, untidy"— bull dike. Not in so many words. Doubt if, for instance, elderly female relatives will think the article any harm, except "she believes in individual freedom, up to and including free love and legalized homosexuality." He didn't write down my recommendation of drinking rights for Indians, no, he chose, the baby fink, he chose the details: black Volkswagen, mannish clothes, straight hair, flat shoes, heavy ring (not signet Mr. Fink, a Welsh mourning ring), nicotine stains, warts, and self-importance. Serves you right. Sarah, out of one unwashed morning, out of an hour impatient for notoriety, you have become this gross pretentious female, able to announce the enormity: you are one of the few intellectuals in Toronto.

I wish I had the kind of mother who'd phone and say "Sarah, don't drink in the morning." Instead, Rosie calls with another sort of blast, not as succinct. She goes on, on... disgrace, indiscretion, inconsiderateness (as if I had something to do with the day it appeared). Angered, I call the paper: "Since we have been good enough to insert an obituary, since Porlock is really not a common name..." Well, there is no one there to take my anger and humiliation. Eldon instead storms in, Peg's fat man, "Sarah, this really will make a lawsuit, it's either that or you'll be laughed out of town." Ridicule, hatred, contempt? Who cares? I want to know.

Our lawyer is amused, remembering in line with this the time I tried to change my name to "Bastard," doubts an important case is here. It is he who says, "Quit drinking in the morning, Sair. That's the funniest thing I've ever read in the *Star*."

Joe phones, to feel my mood. He has taken an apartment high in an expensive tower, furnished Scandinavian, sort of, and, waiting for the hour to bring Ruth to another kind of cell, read about me. "I feel like a tatty fool," I say. "You should." "Eldon wants me to sue." "Eldon suspects you are more famous than you are. Most of the students have gone home. It won't hurt you."

You will, I want to say, but I can't, because I know he wanted living with me to go on, he wanted not to have to face this regeneration of Ruth, he wanted not to leave my snug. "You'd better take some of the pictures, Joe. I'm going to sell the rest."

"No memories," he answers, "are allowed on either side."

What good are leaky rubbers in the rain?

"Listen, did you leave me the bottle of rye?"

"Yes."

I think, now, the only poetry is lists. Funeral, home, corpse, casket, chastisement, IBM, sympathy, lawyer, rest.

II

Sunday, and the pubs are closed. Down where I live, we are not provident. The men pace the streets and alleys restless for brew. We are a park and three houses from relative respectability; livelier, this side, what with the brothel and the police motorcycles providing night entertainment (32B, 32B call at 712 Maitland, how do you spell McGuigan?) and the fights to watch, and the bums spending desperate days before the hostel opens. Now Joe is gone, I am glad to be going myself, though some of the neighbors are fine. Not many from this street go regularly to work, the rest decorate the corners, and have to be passed. The Carpenters' Union on a robin-throated night is a gauntlet to run, even for me. I cannot wipe middle class off my face, and am ashamed as well as half frightened.

Sadly and originally, the street was a carriageway between two parks. It is lined with elms and chestnuts; the houses are large, once-gracious, now rabbit warrens of the poor. My English great-aunts lived on the street in the 1860's, not in this house, perhaps in number eighty-seven, the sole *virgo intacta*, where somebody's great-aunts still live, and tend, determinedly, their lawns and bluebird windows. But it can't have been fashionable for more than ten years, the center of town was two blocks west by the seventies, and our only aristocratic remain is the name of the scrofulous alley: Glenholme Place. This morning, the length of Glenholme Place, a couple my parents' age staggered and swore, he holding her every six paces against a wall and slapping at her. "Kill me, that's right, kill me, you fucking bastard, go ahead, get the razor out of my purse, kill me." She took his blows with a twitch of habit.

Yet I think these people are less corrupt than I am.

Last week Eldon sat on my second-hand sofa, Eldon, husband of Peg, and informed me how to restore my reputation. This was after the interview with Dr. Lyle.

I hated to go to Lyle. When I was an undergraduate, I loved her: she was what I wanted to be. Toronto, McGill, Lady Margaret Hall. Specialist in Spenser. Never said anything rubbishy, dressed like a genteel horse, saw through your superficialities into your virtues; and when I had been through a less distinguished mill, saw fit two years ago to hire me. Principal of St. Ardath's now, a woman of integrity, vision, a genuine and quiet position in public life. All that one could desire.

"Listen," I wanted to say, "don't make any speeches, Gertie, I resign. Save yourself pain." I wanted to speak like this to save myself the pain of sincerity. To throw my resignation down, run, before I could see the disappointment in her eyes. But she was too good to be referred to as Gertie, and I couldn't bring myself to say that by her I no longer wanted to be understood. She was the closest I have come to knowing Jesus, and there was nothing to do but stand there and receive compassion.

"This is a most unfortunate article, Sarah."

"Yes, I'm desperate about it." Or should be.

"You've had a very trying term."

"I have handled it badly."

"There are times when one does." I kept wishing she had some meat on her bones. She's thin, Lyle, and fifty, and when she washes her hair and has it put in sausage curls you know that this is her gesture toward femininity, like my eye goo: acceptance of the hairdresser, of the cosmetic, without acceptance of the world of the product. Her eyes, like that reporter's, are boiled, her body as rimless and self-effacing as her spectacles, as conspicuous because of it. Her ringless hands are dry. No age, shape, definition: all brains and standards. In impersonal circumstances, a delight.

I could not help shifting under her honest eyes, though I had never since I graduated seen reason to imitate her nun's probity; one is, or one isn't, made for the world. I doubt she is stupid enough to expect this; only discretion. But now it was a kind of sacrilege to confront her; when I looked into her eyes I had seen, lately, only a celestial backside in the Adriatic.

"I imagine you expect me to resign," I told her.

Flapping her eyelids back, she said there was no reason I should.

I gave her the old words about teachers influencing the young. "Besides, it will make it hard for you," I said.

"I think it is a mistake to allow a woman's private life, however distasteful it is to me, to interfere with her career more than it would in a man's case." Clearly, she thought I was pregnant. I wondered if she knew a good abortionist. There's a gutsy side to Lyle that doesn't show often, but it's there.

"Do you think you ought to stand up for me?"

"Sarah, Sarah, you've never been able to distinguish between personality and principle. Before the high court of all angels I could not defend your moral position. On the other hand, you have done your work well."

I looked down at my feet to see if I was still wearing patent-leather Mary Janes. But I thought I should have a last crack at honestly reaching her. "I would rather," I said, "that you attacked the superficiality of my teaching. You know it's staginess, flamboyance. I couldn't do it without a gown."

"Sarah, what has happened to you?"

"I'm beginning to see what is honest for me."

"And you think you are not an honest teacher?"

"I'm a natural teacher in a theatrical sort of way. It's been in the family for generations—my mother taught, her mother taught. But I care less and less about my subject, I might as well be teaching kindergarten. It has become going on stage three times a day."

"Your choice of thesis was unfortunate. It led away from scholarship."

"I wanted to see what kind of writing could be done here."

"You care about that, don't you? You're impatient to get on with your own writing."

"If it were so easy!" Does she have bat's or angel's eyes? It is important to feel that someone understands even a corner of you; yet there is always too much compassion in her, as if I am not going to succeed.

"You put me in a difficult position," she says. "I have to demand the best from my staff."

"I know."

"Since you returned from Europe you have seemed disappointingly cynical, preoccupied with yourself. I thought this would disappear when your time of adjustment was over..."

She let the words dangle in a way I was familiar with. It meant she could not see me as a genuine sinner, that I would return to right paths soon enough. And she seemed in that moment as obscene as sterilized milk and sanitized socks, all the good human shit removed, like the writers who kept dying in the ten-dollar anthologies. "I've written out my resignation, Dr. Lyle."

Her sigh was a good meaty one. I was going to be hard to replace, she had known me ten years. "Sarah, you are throwing away a fine career."

"There are scriptural parallels. And I'm making it easier for you. I think you'd eventually have to let me go."

It was natural for her to throw up her hands. "Easy? Your generation has gone so wrong, so wrong. Everything must be easy!"

"I only mean to keep you from being embarrassed."

"I wish you had not stayed so long abroad."

"This would have happened to me here. I wasn't

cut out for the academic. I'm probably just a high
school teacher."

"We don't hire at a low standard here, you know. I
wish you'd reconsider. You are jumping to the conclu-
sion that after what has happened we can't want you.
It is as if you were an undergraduate asking us to fail
you. But I have been pleased with your teaching—in
the first-year course—and I am, in spite of my appear-
ance, in favor of individualism on the part of the staff.
I should have been prepared to fight very hard with
the board to keep you, Sarah. Let us hope you are only
going through a difficult time."

Not yet, that menopause.

"Won't you apply for leave of absence?" She stared
at me and I knew how good she was, how I could no
longer work for her, my world having burst into symbols and she on the wrong side. "No," I said, and
thanked her, and went back to my office, to my own
empty life. I sat at my desk and figured how much I
could sell my books for, the expensive Oxford ones.
They were a bloody pretense, I was up to the Home
University Library and not much else. Not much use
knowing every Australian and Canadian novelist up to
1959 when the critical framework has dissolved and
the necessity of knowing is dubious. Scat, books; scat,
Sarah. Go find a place where you belong.

There are men I want to castrate. Why should
Eldon McBreen's rumbustious balls give him an initiative I lack? Take him to the vet, that's what I'd do,
have him fixed, remove the bits that allow him to

patronize me. He'd dominate too, if he got a chance; I may have no sense, but I have taste. I'm a snob in fact, can't stand the world's Eldons. Take him away.

He was new to St. A's when I came back, twenty months ago. Was from one of the western universities, fat physiologist with a waxed mustache, and the swagger of a man with his way to make. The only good chair in the faculty room is the only one big enough for him, people waited twenty years for Murdo Macdonald to die, just to sit on that chair, along comes Eldon. I built castles on him the minute I saw him, and was right.

We are given lives, and when we are seven or nine or eleven, we begin to decide what we want to do with them. Whether our egos need to become somebody, or are content to go fishing. Walking along railway tracks, teaching yourself to whistle, defending your monstrous egotism against monstrous attack, Fatty, Big Shoes, Lady Jane, Grace-Grace-dressed-in-lace, Smarty-Smarty, George-Porge, and Silly Old Bert, you all compound your dreams, unaware that already they are confined to a pattern. So I, dreamer who never learned to stop, seeing Eldon, saw also a stout slow boy in borrowed clothes becoming a stout, slow professor in second-hand ulster and squashed hat, the larva of the performance in him from birth. He had had, no doubt, a rough childhood; was, and this was part of my dream, and came true, probably illegitimate. The more defenses then, more pretenses later. (Bullies, on the contrary, seldom become anything. Catalysts at ten, they are ciphers at twenty.)

I came, I saw, I disliked. Names bother me, and Eldon is a hell of a farmer's name. Fat bothers me, as if this surfeit of flesh is catching. Why should I be tolerant? My own fatuousness is hard enough to live with—spare me others'.

But Eldon would not spare me. He was oppressively friendly, in spite of my sourness. I was relieved to find it was my sister Peg he was interested in but when they announced their engagement I dreamed of bursting him with a pin.

It was a St. Ardath's wedding, Peg being attached to the biology department, and I, they said, would be bridesmaid. Peg, thirty-four and about three hundred days, five feet tall and a hundred pounds, wants me, four times her size and thinking myself thank God round the coyness corner, wants me to waltz up the chapel aisle, darkening a well-closed door, in pink peau-de-chagrin, endorsing this enormous union. Conjunction of horse and deer, sealed with a tea party, the groom to have a shave and wear a carnation the shape of his right-hand testicle. When I attempted to explain that one acquired the letters Ph.D. after one's name chiefly in order to avoid occasions like this, besides, I couldn't stand Eldon, the usual pious wish for my return to sanity was shouted from rooftops. I flew to Barbados the week before the wedding, where Sandro happened to be dredging. The resulting abortion was expensive and demoralizing, and I dared not take the satisfaction of explaining how their nuptials were celebrated. So when Eldon came to depress my sofa, Eldon like a baboon all behind, talking the glories of the academic, I had things to hold against him.

He made sucking sounds as he drank my rye, and I thought he was going to pee in his pants his gut stuck out so far. "Sarah, you're throwing your job away."

"What's it to you, Eldon?" The ruder I was, the less he seemed to notice.

"It is no concern of mine; I'm upset for your mother."

"You mean I should stay till I get kicked out just to please Mother? I'm thirty. Now, I go gracefully."

"I don't know what you're talking about. You'll have tenure after next year."

Tenure. A long lease on St. Ardath's College, University of Toronto. In thirty-five years I'll be able to retire. The walls started to waver. "I can't," I moaned, with sincerer gestures than I meant him to see. "I can't go on being Jesus in this ghastly place."

Forgot he was an ardent Christian, school of the United Church, as I had been at fourteen. Forgot his powers of indignation. "Jesus! The way you carry on, living like this, taking a good man away from his wife, running off for dirty weekends when you get bored, drinking like a fish, spewing your cynicism into the newspapers and you have the gall—Sarah, you're out of your mind."

Scared for a moment, the idea of insanity is not one I like, every man his own brain surgeon. Still, is he worth my explanations? "I feel," I tried, "as if every time I pass through the gates, every day I work for Lyle, I am more obliged to be what I cannot be, a saintly, serious, kind, and undiscriminating woman. For this I was not made, and it is squeezing me dry."

"I notice it squeezed Joe's wife into a clinic."

"She was that way before he married her."

"There is no justification for you."

"On your terms, no."

"If you made the slightest effort to improve..."

"To do what? 'To be the kind of girl that God would have me be?'"

"Don't make mockery of religion," he thundered.

"Don't muck about in my life."

"Sarah, what happened to you in Europe?"

"You didn't know me before I went."

"No, but I was beaten over the head with the image of this wonderful, bright, intelligent, gorgeous Sarah, light of all our lives, universal favorite, everything a woman should be and a Ph.D. to boot."

"She's a legend." It gave me the creeps to think they talked blindly about me, that way. "And now you see a cynical, formless, immoral wretch. Didn't you ever take lectures from anyone whose catchphrase was 'The truth of course lies somewhere in between'?"

He looked at me hard and I sank for a moment, afraid he knew about Sandro. "Sarah," he said, "you'll have to make a reckoning."

"That's what I'm doing."

"When you've finished you might tell us what you conclude."

"Why you? Why the family? This is my own, one, true life."

"Sarah, we love you."

In addition to lecturing on physiology or whatever venous, venomous stuff it is, Eldon has a television program, where, twice a week, we have the pleasure of his looking us convincingly in the eye for fifteen minutes and asking us to make up our minds on some earth-shaking issue like the moral value of fluoride in water, or music in pubs. He has only one expression, that of a rather stupid basset hound making sure of his supper. He turned it on me and said "We love you." I wanted to puke.

"I don't think I understand that kind of love," I said.

"You belong to the family. We want to see you happy and well."

As far as I knew, my sisters had, feeling their awkwardness in my iconography, been longing for years for my exit. Not to admit it, of course, for we pretend to love each other, stick together, etc., or some of us do. But surely, they too had ceased to live in the innocent Eden past that never existed, the pre-Freud world that even Mother at her best rejects. "We love you," sez Eldon. I would give him F-minus for choice of words.

I speak very slowly in that voice you use for seven-year-olds. "Listen," I say. "I am selling up, going away, fucking off. You may never have a chance to horn in on my reckoning. And if you think we all love each other, I would advise you to look into your own very simple concept of love. My sisters and I are atavistically inclined to stick together when it does us any good. Otherwise, we are a hopeless crew of misfits, like most families. Quit romanticizing. There's a dark side to everything."

He stodges himself further into the chesterfield, pulling at his pipe: postures of reflection and defeat. I realize he is completely opaque. I might have tried to

like him, but my likings of men are dangerous to myself.
A few true things I could keep in my head and use for
or against him—that it is never right to dismiss people,
never right to judge: these I learned here, not in France.
On the other hand, there is also a matter of time, which
ticks away as you suffer fools gladly, and standards,
which melt while you congratulate the painter-by-num-
ber and the genius in plasticine. Eldon wiggled and
winced, I turned off sympathy, told him to go.

His final words: "I hope you are not going back to
Europe. It is bad for you."

"Eldon, go away and read Henry James."

It was not spring enough yet; he shuffled off,
pulling his ulster around him, old and slack. I no
longer wanted his balls, but I would rather, now, hate
than pity. I have heard people say that this country
needs more men like Eldon, self-made, responsible,
concerned, and people who say such things are right.
Except physically, he is perfectly designed for the protection of the status quo, giving his articulateness gen-
erously to support the decisions of authority, offering
up his bastardy to the criticism of such minor flaws in
society as can be acknowledged without disturbing
the long colonial sleep. With men like Eldon at the
wheel, our inner lives can slip quietly away and leave
us emptily in peace. I began to know that my reasons
for going were good.

The bereaved is subject to visitations. Ma's loss,
my gain; but Joe can't fill the fat man's ugly dent in the
chesterfield. Has only an hour to spare. At seven, on

time, he returns to Ruth.

At heart he is as cheerful as a bloodhound. A friend now, emaciated friend, handsome in the old, neurotic, high-bridged way, and pale from a sunless, overworked winter, pale from his high, bare forehead to his pleasurable long hands, which I will not see on me again. Return to Ruth is serious; if he is to save her he must be her personal missionary for the rest of their lives, refuse to be driven when she pelts him away. That she should become his one patient is her only hope.

I remember Ruth in Paris: one of the insect-girls I envied, small, beat, do-anything girls, this one with frizzy black hair, a smile I wouldn't have called reckless. Free, Joe said, free. Wild, certainly, in the American-in-Paris way, and clever with her hands, barefoot girl with jar of morning-glory seeds, one of the lot who made odds and ends of modernistic jewelry out of stones. I could see her bent over some cowboy, squeezing blackheads. A brown corduroy Ginsberg Girl, and thin. One night she took us on to the *quais* to a pot party—guitars, jeans, and an Algerian with supplies. Nobody offered me any, but Joe smoked and leaned on me, wrote an article later on her and her set.

I'd like to think it was Toronto made her sick, being brought from Paris, and the shock of being plunged back into what your mother's generation in America was running away from. But I saw her a couple of times in her tantrums—pot, seeds, Old Sailor, any way to oblivion, and only Ruth and life did that to Ruth. Choosing the ruinous pressures.

What's left of her is quiet, accepting as a child, nothing to do with the old, wild Ruth of Paris.

But we've all changed since the *wanderjahre*.

France was a crisis for me. It came after five years based unsteadily on a week of provincial narcissism. Somebody says what will you do your graduate work on, I think, Our Land, Our Lit., ways to extend it. So I spend five years, three in London on a stipend narrow as a nun's bed, learning ever more deeply to hate *Voss* and *Two Solitudes*. Equating poverty with honesty, I was sure I was doing good work. Ugly on abstractions, stodge, and shilling-fed water heaters, not worried about lank hair, I finished the exams, then the thesis, and a Foundation was found to send me to meet certain savants on the subject of Africa, French colonial effusion. Wearer of woolly vests, eater of chips, I cross the channel, grubbily, and into shock.

I can't say that I lived in England—rather, I inhabited what I came to regard as a series of portable bed-sitting rooms, each one like the other, though cheaper, and gradually reduced my possessions to two suitcases, which could be left at stations when one was fleeing the rent collector. I felt at home there, it was one perpetual "grubby day," once I got used to doing without baths, and my feet got broader to meet the exigencies of cheap English shoes, and my ankles got thicker, and my legs got those red circles from always being cold. And of course my face was spotty, my Canadian clothes were replaced by Marks and Sparks', I became sordid-English faster than anyone I know. Train-soiled, you might say, unpressed; but I felt a part of it all.

It was easy enough to see in France how much I had become a part of it all. I spent two weeks in darkest Brittany and even there *"vous Anglo-Saxon"* was thrown haughtily at me. But I had lived three years in such isolation, such a small, intellectual world, with my bed-sits, theater queues, reading-room ticket, cans of sardines, France was a shock. Suddenly, a snobbery that accepted me as possible of improvement (in London one was patently "out" and alone) insisted on sybaritic baths. I removed layers of felt from my flesh, pitched my voice high, and spoke of myself, soon, in the feminine gender. *"Oh-la-la,"* I heard myself saying to my hostess Martine. *"L'Angleterre."* She agreed. France is the only country whose magazines publish "after" pictures that are real improvements on "before."

In Paris, Joe took me ungrudgingly from the Celtique to the Monaco to the Échaudé and the Cinémathèque, someone from his past to explain things to, such as at which hour one moved from the Dôme to the Sélect. I was the largest member of his *petite bande* of stone-jeweled and sticky beatniks, out-of-work architects, film directors, and journalists. I thought at the time they'd be out of place in the British Museum, and no one got up till the museums were practically closed, but with them I felt relatively honest, relieved a little of the humiliation of failing before France; but in no state to absorb myself in Joe.

I almost decided, after a fortnight, not to go south. These were the days of the Nouvelle Vague, there was a chance of a party at Belmondo's, things were happening. I found a hotel in the rue de la

Parcheminerie called "Le Grand Hotel Robinson," buttressed by telephone poles, scrofulous, full of Algerians. I wanted to live there, around the corner from St. Julien-le-Pauvre. It was satisfying to think of, abandoning oneself to the city, to Joe's circle, folk songs, cafés, and *vernissages;* but then, at the pot party, I felt Joe sliding toward Ruth. I needed my English underwear, sitting on cold stones. I was old in my bones, among the guitars, old, old. There was a professor to see in Aix-en-Provence who knew about Gabon and the Cameroons. I thought Joe might help me decide, but when I went to ask he had Ruth clutched in his bed. I took the sixty-three bus to the Gare de Lyon. In a way, I have never come back north.

Late in November, I read Joe's wire over my breakfast tray, lolling against my bolster in the alcove of *toile de jouy*. The maid hustled in with the second round of coffee, and flung open the shutters. *"Et maintenant, petite Sarah, il faut vous lever."*

"Arrive Marseille 4:45, explore Provence Joe."

It was my day to meet the Professor, at four o'clock on the dot, but what the hell, Joe was an old friend, Joe was Joe, I canceled, beginning the end of my academic career.

Station its mess of usual excitement: Friday, full of wet Algerians, Greeks getting off the train carrying beds. And Joe comes tearing down the concourse all new light, sweeping me into his arms, I look wonderful, he's sold a story to *The New Yorker*, we must see Aix, God it's going to be as wonderful as Spain, have I got any money, we ought to have a ball, man, a ball.

Impressed by his geniality, Madame my landlady

sets another place at the dinner table, makes sure that he takes an expensive hotel room across the street. He spreads a charm I haven't seen in him before, praises the food and the cats, eats boiled leeks vinaigrette without a grimace, commends the wine. The maids, the landlady, the female *pensionnaires* all pretend to be overwhelmed, raising their hands like puppets, with false smiles, trying to decide if he's a queer because they think I'm a Lesbian, cosseting him. The two Etonians giggle at his halting and un-British French, are envious of his second helping of floating island. I am inclined to be on their side, for at enormous expense I have made this house my territory, and I do not want next week to be lauded only for knowing Joe. It is rather like a family visit at summer camp, when one hates one's mother's charm.

When I get him into the country, I think, the tables will turn. I've been here six weeks, hardly ever still, I know the territory. And his unnerving high spirits can't last, something will bring back his old, quiet gloom.

Madame of course wants to know our plans, and he has them. You wouldn't think he'd heard of Ginsberg or the Monaco, he's very much the *New Yorker* man for her sake, and tells her about taking tea with Alice B. Mentions, too, too casually (oh, this country is giving me hawk's eyes) a friend of a friend in Paris, a certain Countess who lives near the Ste. Baume. Madame is beautifully human, loves a scandal, loves a title. The Countess gives parties—receptions for businessmen who want to impress their friends. We must get in touch at once, if Joe knows Madame de Pradier, they huddle obscenely over her book of addresses, drafting his letter in glee. I cease to exist, and am jealous; but I have never liked to share.

All through that trip we were like children, all victories over each other. I know Marseille, but my feet get cold and I cough in the outdoor cafés. Joe goes farther abroad and learns the city by perseverance and cheerfulness. Further, with his darkness, he seems less foreign than I do, finds an openness in people that my better accent does not create. I trail behind, sulky and tedious, knowing the insect-girls in Paris were never like this, old.

When we give up the gastronomy of the port for the exploration of the east, we quarrel over hotel rooms; one landlord seems to think I am being abducted (who would?) by my insistence on two beds. I remember that Katherine Mansfield lived here, and D. H. Lawrence died, and anyway, the palm trees are badly tailored, there is a jukebox on the *quai* that has turned the Boy Scout song into rock and roll. The winter rains are plainly made for finishing off consumptives, unheated terrazzo floors freeze my feet, outdoors one is never warm enough, there is a sepulchral chill. In England, you accept this annual martyrdom, but when the rain beats down the carnation stakes of the Midi, resentment sets in. Olives taste wrong in the wet.

By Sanary I am in wildly bad humor. Joe told the Countess to write us at the Beau Rivage, but there is no question of our staying there, we are humped together in a three-foot bed in a pension, noshing on tinned tuna in *vol-au-vent* shells. Joe hums and ignores me. Sunday seems a week long. You can see that in the summer this is a heavenly place; now, trying to concentrate on Penguin paperbacks, I am nagged by the thought of the back country we have not explored, the Giono country; the rosemary will be sopping underfoot. In Aix I have a little green porcelain wood. stove.

On Monday, we count up our francs (he may have sold to *The New Yorker*, or he may not, but he hasn't got the cheque) and decide we have enough for a hot-water bottle and a decent meal. I go out cheerfully, and add to my purchases brandy to guzzle in bed; come in to find Joe poring over a map. The Countess has come through.

God, though, a *thé dansant*. Palm Court orchestras and chiffon? Tomorrow, at seventeen hours, in old spiky handwriting, she announces that she will be delighted to receive the Canadian friends of Madame, at the Château d'Andreu, close to St-Maximin-La-Ste.-Baume. There is no RSVP. We are expected to arrive; given, even, the name of a respectable hotel at St. Maximin where we can dress. "You're smiling," Joe says, "you terrible snob." And bursts into giggles himself.

I like old women, especially in France, where they seem incredibly old and tell you about the Franco-Prussian War. In their eighties old women tell tales of a pleasing tartness: you get suffragettes, corsets, kid gloves, gin rummy, the bad manners of youth, musical evenings, calling cards, taxes, forms of love and loyalty that smell of dried violets and potpourri: things gone now. I turned happily from Colonial literature to Victorian, learning from my old women the why's of Dear Mr. Ruskin, dreadful Léon Blum, and the Pax

Victoriana. Tough old birds, they are, and in France, deliciously corrupt. The *thé dansant* would cost us, but the Countess, from her handwriting and her reputation, was a specimen to study.

All day we were stylized characters, our glazed eyes fixed on the crisis ahead. We counted money, counted hours and possibilities. I was victorious to see Joe as involved in frivolities as I; dreams of castles have been instilled in him too. Tired of waiting for his frog to turn into a princess, he'll take his chance at the Château.

Now, in the distillation of now, on a Toronto Sunday that is longer than any Sunday Sanary could invent, he is in my apartment for a restricted hour, asking guiltily, how can he help?

"I don't need anything, Joe."

"You've given a hell of a lot to me, I'd like to..."

"Forget it. Remember the week before we went to the Château, how I was jealous and ratty and afraid? Think of me like that."

"In those days we expected a lot of each other."

"Emotional crooks."

"I liked you," he protests. "I wouldn't have come to see you unless I did."

"The hell you liked me: I was someone you knew in a place you hadn't been to, that's all."

"We were long in the tooth to be high school sweethearts."

"You had your plans," I accuse him.

"A little idle plotting. And when you were in a good mood you were heaven to travel with."

"So were you: a pair of extra eyes."

"We had good times."

"And when I came back here, and hated it, you were the only one I could talk to. Remember, when Ruth was at home that time, you drove me up to my uncle's in the country?"

Joe remembers, and brings the old man's voice back in affectionate mimicry. "Soyabintayurp, Sarah, soyabintayurp."

III

Yurp is not England, or a weekend's hosteling in the Low Countries, or Sunday at Knokke-le-Zoute, or holding hard onto your change-purse in the Champs Élysées.

Yurp is something dark in Methodists.

It goes from the Bay of Biscay to the Urals, from Scandinavia to Israel. The Holy Land is not Yurp, but Israel is. Ireland is, because of the peasants, but Scandinavia only occasionally. Spain stands alone.

Yurp is composed of wogs, frogs, wops, bohunks, Jews, kikes, huns, dogans, dutchmen, slays, polacks, Greeks, mad Hungarians, Finns, Cyps, salad greens, herbal remedies, and the Iron Curtain.

They are liable to cheat you.

Stay away from the men.

From Yurp came Communism, evolution, catholicism, and sex.

To avoid being European you can be a Parisian or a Viennese or a Venetian, but you can't escape being Italian. And if Swedes are turnips, Belgians are horses, and who eats Swiss chard?

Well, Joe and I were in Yurp. Living, more or less, in sin. Talking, as a matter of fact, of marriage, and that under the unreasonable rain. We had something to do, we were going to Toulon looking for clothes to wear to a *thé dansant*, and he kept talking about marriage and I, stuck in my frame of reference, which is me, kept wondering if he meant me, and crossing it off, and he went on marriage, marriage, what is it? I keep wanting it, he said. I keep looking for some girl to be monogamous with. It hasn't happened to me before, it scares me. Is it just wanting to breed, or get it regular? I'm thirty, Sair, suddenly I want all those things—home, kids, plugged-in affection. Not love, the old thing, roses, moonlight. I've had that. What I want's a good lay after a good supper, someone to bring the bone home to: atavism.

And yet his mother was that hard-drinking rich red-headed slut around the corner, who drank first her reputation, then her husband, her son, and her liver away.

Joe's at least himself again, warm and pessimistic. I edge closer in the vibrating bus. A man talking about himself is as good as in bed.

And why not before? he asks. Never wanted it before. Now, who are my friends? Youngsters and queers. Others all settled, tied down. Dammit, I find myself wanting those ropes. Do you?

Not yet, I say. I get letters from home setting me against it. So and so's lovely children. They smell of milkvomit.

"You will want it."

"Not on those terms. If I could be the man, bring the bone home myself, not raise babies—maybe. But there's too much to do and see. I've been years in prison, Joe."

"You're not lonely?"

"Hellishly."

"Then you must be half Lesbian."

"I don't think so. I'd want to be the aggressor, but it repels me, the thought of touching women. The good thing about men is being under them, subordinated; it gives you a sense of where you belong—biologically and for always. But to be under—and with freedom—only a hell of a good man could give you that. Most of them hate you to think. They have to be over you in all the wrong ways."

"I'm like that."

"No, for a man, you're broad-minded."

"Academic women—brrrr..."

"It's a job, and they'll change when academic grants get big enough to pay for baths."

"Look, Sarah, you're the fool. Always since I've known you, in love with some remote guy you can't marry."

"Protection racket. I want to work for a while yet."

"But eventually?" He was hoping to find me human.

"Yes, I'll get nesty, like the rest, like you."

"When you've got it, freedom is gritty."

Ask me now what is Toulon, I'll tell you, used clothes and the smell of them, Joe worried about marrying: they eat your bread and breed brats, but what else is it? I think the closeness that I want is something no man can have.

Fool, I was rummaging in furnishings and trimmings. I could have turned to him and offered myself, now we would be leading useful lives. But no, I was muddling in a trunk of tatty costumes, looking as usual in the past for Sarah's future. Listen, I should have said, we could have that; we could manage. There's something between us to build on, we've both tried the *grande passion* before, we know it doesn't work for us, it's a waste of emotion to go on looking for it. If we put our defenses aside, Joe, I should have said, if we just lie back and listen for the sounds we know are in us, we can make a life, Joe...

But I was rummaging, and then he started talking about Leah.

"Your sister," he said, "the one they used to call Lotus Blossom, why haven't you looked her up?"

St. A's own Zuleika Dobson thrown in my face again. "The one with the vibrating blue vein in her forehead?"

There was an old woman in a back alley who had caged larks fattening; relict of the theater, she had trunks of dresses and spoke Italianate, oily French. I stood potbellied in her parlor while Joe draped me in rotting silk, crumbling chiffon, and talked Leah.

"She was a legend. There were always fellows who said about you, 'She has this fantastic sister.' And you were jealous."

"God, Joe, I still am."

"There, you've got it done up crooked. Look at this label, it's Worth. That's going a bit far back, isn't it? Let me help. I like dressing women, I used to like undressing my mother, putting her to bed. Nothing

Freudian, just taking care of her." His hands were deft. He smoothed a tube of peach velvet over my protuberances. "There, you look awful. What you need is a little, vibrating vein..."

I wanted to shout "I hate her, I've always hated her, if you want her, go screw her." Instead, I took Worth's weariness off ungently.

Spoke the part of him that is fretful and wistful. "You could be pretty and gentle, Sarah. I wish you wouldn't just settle back and be picturesque."

"Oh, for heaven's sake." The old dress was off and I stood looped in elastics before a parlor pier glass, ugly. Frocks, jackets, stomachers, crowns; tulle and bombazine, mohair and monkey fur, soul-shriving dead velveteen. There had to be something to cover my knobs and my boobs, give me pride, once before tomorrow when I get old; before I am inevitably sealed and packed away in the academic I want once to deceive myself in this direction: become beautiful, vulgarly gorgeous, gross, wanted. So he talks about Leah.

"Don't you even write to her?"

"Christmas cards."

"Didn't she come to see you ever in London?"

"No."

"Why the hell don't you go to Venice?"

"I've been happy since she left, really happy, just knowing she's out of my world. It's demoralizing to be the homely sister."

Having been an only child, he can't understand. "I'd have gone. As a matter of fact I was thinking we could push off to Venice from here."

"Never!"

"Oh, come on, the fare's only ten bucks. We could just camp on her doorstep and have a look at Venice."

"No, Joe. We're not teen-age hitchhikers."

"Oh, all right. Try this." Just a dress, human, quirky, unfashionable and distinguished: cut for a big body, about 1931, a Lanvin label. "That should do." For three minutes Sarah stood and looked at the Sarah in the old pier glass: what she wanted to see. Joe's eyes gleamed, as if he had just met somebody. He stopped talking about Venice.

He was so nice after that, so concerned for me as a woman, I felt obliged to justify. "We weren't twins, Joe, we were two separate sisters; and she can't want me in her life any more than I want her. Our parents didn't know any better, they raced us against each other, rubbed in what the other one was. Besides, going to Venice, it's like going to New York, something to dream about, then do when you have a lot of money. Imagining is easier, it keeps you from being disappointed until the right time. And what would I say, 'Hi, Leah, how's the girl?' We'd turn into our old selves at the first word. You like people, Joe, you'd have liked growing up in a passel of women. But you haven't lived that terrible, narrow, competitive life, reaching for higher things. It was a competition to see who would make the best Lady Jesus."

No comment; wet scenery slides by. "Ruth is like you," he says finally. "She hates hard."

"Ruth?"

"You met her on a motor scooter. The dark girl from New York."

"Oh, her."

"Don't dismiss her, you'll put me off women. She's quite reasonable."

He'll never manage to live with her, I thought, or her sticky neck.

IV

Mood came from the weather, from premonitions of disaster which I have since learned (since I began to shed my education) to trust. I was not surprised to find my shoulder straps slipping; to find that the château was crumbling and moldy in the rain; to find that the furniture had claws.

The butler, however, was a Negro. There are higher taxes on colored servants than on white in France. He, with the three Mercedes, two 403's, one Jaguar, one Porsche on the graveled carriageway, spoke of money somewhere.

The Countess rustled with paid enthusiasm. Her black taffeta had turned green with age, never mind. She was hung with beads and bits of monkey fur and her own long teeth: the genuine, awful article. Courageous, resourceful, desperate, all the clichés: and with it, tatty. Her bird's eyes found us barely satisfactory, but she took us in with resignation, measuring our foreign accents. Joe gave her the mutual friend's formalized greeting and we followed her through the anteroom, which was vaguely eighteenth century with boars' heads and busts, and hadn't been dusted since, into the salon.

I have dined guiltily off this story five times a year since it happened, dined off it, embroidered it, laughed at it, mocked it, set it up for villains and for friends. Never told the truth.

It sits now like a wen on my blotched conscience. Sarah is not the girl she was; truth has aged and been cobbled as well. Not even to myself do I tell it true, now. It has become one of my Funny European Stories.

Well, kid Sarah, that era has ended. You are about to remove yourself from a position whence you can tell Funny European Stories. Say on, and purge.

Begin seriously, then. "The Countess's insouciance gave us new identities; in our hired costumes we were *deux psychologues Canadiens, Mlle. Stella Porter et M. Jean Olivier.*"

Actually, my dress was bought. See what I mean about truth? The true words are often wrong to the ear.

And she was about as insouciant as a hawk. Deaf, rather.

And she didn't introduce us. She mumbled the words and threw us in, stopping without audience because in the middle of the salon there was a good-looking blonde talking about life in Toledo, Ohio. Hair slanting across the forehead, across the flickering blue vein in her forehead.

It was such a shock I didn't do a double take; I pretended instead that it hadn't happened. Suddenly, lurchingly, I was trapped. It was like seeing a lost lover, only worse. Childhood phantoms were rising to strangle me again. I could not even nod. I ducked away from the claws on the Empire chairs.

Leah was fine, perfect for this place, even too good. Her French was faultless, with that feminine gurgle which distinguishes women's French from men's, a pleasant, birdlike repetition of adverbs. *"Pas du tout du tout du tout?"* Dress elegant, and the finesse of small-boned wrists now braceleted in gold. I slid onto a squat chair to listen. The Countess had told them she was from Toledo, Ohio, and she was making the best of it.

I was both detached and in a panic of disappointment. The old ambivalence toward Leah had returned. The threat of her rivalry was, since we were now on completely different levels, diminished; I could now even envy her, for although she was a glorious object, I did not then want her place. She had become one of those women behind whose façade there are hours and hours with the hairdresser, the manicurist, and the seamstress in London, Paris, and New York. A woman like a sleek cat whose beauty depends on patience, finely balanced tension, and an authoritarian household. I could not change chairs with her, even though having children had taken the blank look off her face, even though life in what I presumed was international society had given her a poise I should never achieve. No, she wasn't, any more, what I wanted to be. But she was still a threat.

I looked around for her husband. Which man?

Joe was looking around, too.

Listening, leaning toward Leah, there were fat men, thin men, hunchbacked men and fairy men. An elegant old Vicomte, straight out of Proust, a beautiful violinist I had heard the week before in Aix, very correct and queer. A couple of Germans, a bearded Slav, only the three of us from the new world, no English, the rest apparently French and not particularly distinguished.

What would Mother have thought, I wondered. The whole circle listening raptly to her lying daughter.

The famous Sandro did not seem to be there. He must be large and dark; my parents had met him and called him handsome and refined, if in their view an Italian could be called refined. If refined, then not leaning forward into the words of his wife, not like the Weimaraner-eyed German panting toward her. No, somebody cool, but no one was cool, except the women, who looked bored and a little jealous. Perhaps she had come alone.

If she had seen me come in, and she must have seen me come in, she had not betrayed herself; no flicker of recognition troubled her eyelids. She went on talking, and stopped when she had said enough. She did not seek me out even with her eyes after that. Tonight she wasn't going to know me. Probably here with another man.

Waiters brought weak punch, general conversation was resumed. Neither Joe nor I talked; our eyes were busy. I watched Joe watch Leah.

It was not only a *thé dansant*, it was a *café-concert* as well. A moldy little chamber group filed in and played with a reediness unequaled by Cunard lounge orchestras.

The Countess singled Joe out and moved him somewhere. I felt unprotected and immediately hostile; must concentrate, find a friend. What did I know about Leah's husband: where was the man, big for an

Italian, distinguished for a wop, and intelligent for a foreigner: someone commanding and prosperous enough to turn the hesitant chauvinism of my mother to respect? (My father restricted himself to a feeling of wonder that anyone could cohabit peacefully with any of his daughters.) Probably not here, but surely she doesn't go running around the south of France with stray friends, she was never that independent.

A man behind me, to the left, was looking down my neck. By turning I could look at him; I met a pair of derisive eyes. That was the man, surely. "A psychologist?" he asked slowly, and with amusement.

"Why not?"

I hadn't seen him before. And he was big. He wore a neat little decoration in his lapel, but he was not old. Mid-thirties, perhaps. Commanding, certainly, and prosperous. I shivered and the orchestra slid squeakily into silence. He moved his chair up to me, looked at me with insulting candor and held forward a cigarette. Leah looked at us without interest.

Politely, should I say "So you are Sandro?" No, let him take the initiative. When I feel him looking at me again there will be the sensation that I am starting to swell. Can't one become sixty and truly enormous before that age? Impatient for him to speak, I shift on my seat, kid beginning to swell under the pedagogical eye.

"So you dislike men?"

There's a beginning that is also an end. "I hate being stared at." Feed it right back.

"My apologies. I was unaware... but you have an interesting face."

The stare was an old maid's dream, I still go to call it "blatantly sexual," I'm still not so far from spinster's salivations; nonsense, it was an evaluation. Woman being summed up, as woman, cuisine included as well as sex, health, cleanliness, brain, temper, fingernails. How would it be to know this one? Lead through strength, I told myself. "Do you know people here?" Maybe it was the first conversation I had calculated since my first conversation.

"My wife, and a few others."

"It's a funny party."

"For business people."

"Yes?"

"A number of us have been seeking a contract for work on one of the family properties."

"One should consider it an honor to be included, then."

"It is quite normal to invite foreign students of good family."

So he gave me something. "What sort of business are you in?"

"Oh, a little building, a little shipping. Nothing important." Apparently he was with the women's magazines in considering my question rude. "Are you alone?"

"I came with a friend, but the Countess took him off."

"Ah yes, a thin and intelligent man."

"I suppose so."

"Is it not true, then?"

Either he was onto something, or he collected women. I felt large and disgruntled. Parties at châteaux should not include inquisitorial eyes—or should they? More likely I was the element that did not fit. "Yes, very intelligent."

"And very boring?"

"Not at all. We are very good friends, and I dislike boring people."

"Sometimes they have their solid qualities."

So he was a moralist. There was no reason to answer him. He was not my old uncle. Instead, I leaned forward into the musicians' renewed scrapings, caught Leah flashing him some sort of message. Superior bastard, I thought as he excused himself, but well tailored. Thought he was in diving and salvage. I needed either a drink or Joe. Of course I could have slipped over to Leah and created a family reunion, but the claws on the furniture said no.

I have tried hard for a long time not to believe in Love At First Sight, never wanted to give so much away so quickly (though I do all the time), learned from adolescent and terrible crushes on distant basketball players that this was pain and humiliation. You have to be simple, to love well, you have to have a sense of humor, your world has to be steady enough not to slide off the peaks of exultation; otherwise and dear Lord not again, you find yourself on your knees to some man, some poor opaque man who wants a lighthearted affair instead of eternity, or worse still some serious and understanding man who cannot stand the weight, envisage himself ravaged by this thick-lipped passion. Not my road, this kind of love.

But there are, alas, affinities; most not to be ashamed of. Moments when you meet someone and it is as if he put a finger in your mouth and touched the red survivor of the tonsillectomy; sometimes, it is like this with a woman, too, although more as if she had touched your mere experience. It means something, it means that there can be something between you if you do not, with reason, run away. Over the years I have got good at running away, though less willing as the fruity urges of thirty commandeer my strength.

So there was a sudden close feeling I did not want to analyze. Because of this, furthermore because he was imperious, there was hostility. And because he was married to Leah. Yet I wanted to know him. In personal legend he was the fisherman who pulled my sister out of the sleeping sea. What did he do with his mermaid? How did a mermaid turn into a wife? Now they were under my eyes I was no longer diffident, wanted badly to find a way of talking to them.

So you see, I tell at dinner, the old lady introduced us all by the wrong names, and there weren't many people one could talk to, so I wound up dancing with this tall character all evening, Leah being busy with Joe, whom she pretended to keep in the dark, and a thin blond sod she seemed to have brought with her. She circulated among the men the way she used to at school dances, a very pure blonde, cat-eyed icicle. I danced with the Countess's grandnephew who was on leave from the Algerian war and hated the world, but most of the time with the tall man my brother-in-law, until it began to seem that both of us knew who we were. Though Leah always liked games.

Most of the Italians I had met before were four feet tall, the sort that clutch you hard on the dance floor, thrust one leg between your two, and bury their faces in your breasts. Sandro was of course not like this, but he made intimacies with his fierce eyes and was not flattering. I was under a microscope. "I should like to meet your wife," I said.

At eight, there was an interval for food—a meager banquet of dry cakes, weak punch, the heralded tea. The Countess was making economies. Joe found me at the table, introduced with a wink that Mme. Leonie Bragance whom the Countess had led him to—and her husband, Alexandre. Stella Porter and Jean Olivier were very polite. The four of us, in fact, murmured memorized idioms with withdrawn courtesy, ready to laugh when there was a chance. Leah appeared to be preoccupied with the violinist, and amused at my dress. Joe's eyes were glued to her goddam blue vein.

Oh, this evening, it went on. Ought to have ended at nine, but the Countess was flushed and let the band play. Perhaps her contractors were dealing successfully in the coat cupboard, needed their wives amused for another hour. Indeed, the men appeared to be thinning, and I found myself alone on the terrace among the potted lemon trees with Sandro, a maneuver I could not have managed had I plotted it. I had a terrible longing for truth—or a drink.

"You are very impatient."

"Yes."

"And, in spite of what you have said, rather bored."

"No. But it's not an important party."

"What is important?"

"Oh, ideas, relationships—things that happen."

"And nothing has happened tonight?"

"Not yet."

"You sound rather wicked."

"What I mean is, I want a drink."

"Do you drink a lot?"

"When I drink. I am a puritan, after all."

It was both damp and freezing. Was the occasion worth pneumonia? I kept hoping that if I stayed out of the claustrophobic little ballroom I would feel sane again. "Let me fetch you some punch—Miss Porter."

"I'd rather not. French rum is dreadful."

Not promising social conversation. I was having to play the man-hater more than before. While we were dancing he had subjected me to a sly interrogation, skirting the subjects of birth and relationship, leaving obvious blanks. I had lied as far as it amused me to do, wondering whether Ma's weekly letters to Venice were as exhaustive as her missives to Aix. But I'm a bad liar, my talent is for telling the truths that no one believes. I ought to have asked him questions—where do you live, how many children do you have?—but every time I forced one out, the answer was so expected that I was thrown again; and with all this he looked at me quizzically, as if I were a new specimen, unlabeled.

"Do you love the man you are with?"

"He's an old friend."

"I think he is the wrong sort of person for you."

"Why?"

"He is too intellectual, too weak."

"He is extremely good company." Annoying that he presumes to opinions already. He must know who I am, and what is there behind that long, and not very Italian, rather cavalier's, face? Intelligence, surely, but not honesty. A true Venetian. For the first time but not the last I looked at him bitterly and was glad I had found out that his ancestor Bragadino had been flayed alive at Famagusta. I promised myself a pilgrimage to the skin.

"I think you can be a very amusing person," he said. "I think you like to laugh and drink wine, not to be shut up in museums. Why are you determined to be sad tonight?"

Because, damn it, I'm busy plotting the moves in this game, and I'm no good at games. "Oh, I'm not in a good mood."

"In that case, I shall leave you to your thoughts. Perhaps your young man will come back to you."

Alone out there, I shivered and chewed my nails. It reminded me of harrowing double dates with Leah in high school, the extra man trailing me in my Oxfords and watching the blue vein; Leah mute, Sarah telling aimless, nervous stories, and at the end, Leah raising her sealed mug insolently, saying, "It's not true. Everything she says is a joke." And producing quite another version. I could see her now dancing with Sandro, giving him just such a look as I had suffered from at six. She has power, that girl, I thought, and she knows how to use it. But she only pretends to be a fool.

Joe appears. "You look miserable."

"Sorry, gracious ladies should smile. Amusing yourself?"

"The blonde's a Canadian, too."

"I keep meeting Canadians."

"Smile, and I'll dance with you. It's nearly over."

All four of us were playing the game hard.

The Countess was whirling in a waltz with a little hunchback, one the nephew had described proudly as *"un vrai fin de race."* The baron *de* something, impotent, crippled, stammering, owner of one of the best collections of pictures between Aix and St.-Tropez. They made a wonderful couple, a couple of caricatures out of Dickens, though without a moral. Time went on, the race became bent, the money ran out, all that was left was taste, green silk, monkey fur. Our game was unreal next to theirs.

At last the band packed up. There was a kind of receiving line to run through before we packed up. As we thanked the Countess for her expensive and unsatisfactory entertainment, our French was as thin and tired as her energy. Her attention was reserved for the businessmen. *Thé dansant*, I muttered, and sealed tenders. For her, a brave new world. I smirked and was clapped on the shoulder from behind.

"You are tired?"

"A little, thank you."

"This isn't a late night for a scholar."

Come off it, buster, let me go. "Where are the coats?"

"The butler will have them." He moved over to Joe. "You are staying at St. Maximin? My wife and I would be pleased if you and Miss Porter would join us for supper before you return."

We hadn't dared think of how to get back to the hotel except by hitchhiking. This indignity spared us, our last pretense was to disguise our raincoats as we waited under the boar's head in the hall for Sandro and

Leah to join us. Odious Joe was preening himself. "Listen," I said, "you know who they are."

"Should I?"

"Do you want to?"

"I suppose truth will out."

"Well you know damn well it's Leah and her husband, I'm sick, sick, sick of this game."

"Don't lose your temper."

Leah joined us, smooth as cream. Their car was one of the Mercedes, of course. As we got into it the château died for us all.

Sandro knew a village where the food and wine had the tang of discovery without being humble (Sandro does not like humility) and the toast was "To my sister-in-law, who shall now be called Stella." The relief made us laugh, and drink more, and the four of us, especially the two of us, got on splendidly, as they say, and on the way to our luggage we contracted for Christmas in Venice.

Bien passé.

And this time, the truth.

V

Truth being that action for Sandro is the raising of an eyebrow; for Porlocks endless confirming letters; and a man stumbles out of the booze can blinded by his bleeding head, cracks it on the sidewalk at the bottom of the steps. Class does exist.

In return for our Leah, Sandro laid at our feet his finesse and authority. While we were still in that vacant, glazed summer assessing according to our jealousies his audaciousness, a letter arrived which removed him from category Wop (people who devalue real estate) to category Our Venetian Son-in-law. In English both idiomatic and respectful, he begged forgiveness for his impulsiveness; set Father's mind at rest by explaining the terms on which the Consul would endorse the marriage, and announced that until the marriage took place, Leah was staying with the Consul himself in Toronto. Congratulated, further, our parents on having produced such a model of womanly behavior. Appended newspaper clippings explaining that a representative of the registered company Bragadino, Rocca, S.R.L., of Milan and Venice, was supervising oil surveys in the Great Lakes. Since no one stood more in awe of Big Business and

Government Officials than Porlocks, they pretended to forget he was a Catholic. And in Venice I saw further evidence of his astuteness: he had removed from one of the articles he sent a paragraph mentioning his relationship with the then Cardinal Roncalli.

Headshaking ceased. Mother would like to have gone to the wedding; Father adopted Sandro's authority and told her to wait until she was invited, which she was not. We never found out whether Leah was churched, or where. One more out of the nest, they decided, and in the hands of a strong and respectable man. Wops and Cathlicks became forbidden subjects, replaced by picture books on Italian art.

Authority and finesse: Sandro and Leah at the little inn. "And you will both come to us for Christmas?"

Leah asks if I am still working on my doctorate, if I am glad I kept on. "Dr. Sarah Porlock," she murmurs. Joe smiles up at me. With such a name what can one be but fat?

"I'm thinking of changing it."

"Getting married?" Sandro asks.

"God, no. I'd like to find if it is legal to change it to Sarah Bastard."

"Why not?"

"There's probably a regulation about suitable names. You know Canada."

Leah gives me her little cold appraising look. "It's a show-off name, Sair."

"I have to do something."

"Divine discontent," Joe murmurs.

"But honestly, Porlock..."

"No," says Sandro, "it will make your life too complicated. You will always be explaining yourself to petty officials..."

"I've got the time."

"Oh, you shouldn't have, then. And when you marry..."

"She doesn't need to marry," Leah cut in, "she has her doctorate."

I began to like her. "But you have two sons," I blustered.

"Anybody can have kids. You're free." There was an excitement in her eyes—what she would do with her freedom. I looked quickly at Sandro, who was staring not at his wife, but at me, trying to read my looks.

"In five years," he said, "you'll be so distinguished we shall not know you."

"You can have a very wonderful life." My sister's voice is colorless in English now, and languid, too many years of talking English for Foreigners have made the cadence forced.

A very wonderful life. The dust and ashes of my personal reality glitter in her mind. Sandro reads me: "You know, I can see you two in each other's places, Leah with spectacles, an attache case, a beautiful tweed suit, reading over a lectern. And Sarah was built to be in a kitchen. As careers, the kitchen and the university are *passionants*."

I could have told him which of the two wasn't; because tonight more than ever I knew I was in the wrong place. The accomplishments of Leah were the reality. She had effaced home and become a personage from Henry James, moving on from the study of the texts to the living of them, although one later came to doubt that she would make her own text. She had, however, banked her shrewdness in a more real institution than the one I was connected with, and though when I contemplate the diaper service and the installment plans which govern my friends' lives, I am happy enough to be what I am, beside Leah I feel like a poor Story.

"You must come to us for Christmas," this Sandro she has taken repeats over the cognac, and I assent dumbly. I know he is right, for the lives of sisters are part of a serial compulsively read.

News from the motorcycles of the alleyway. Someone calling for Bill shatters a bottle against a wall. Across the street a row of Chinamen in rocking chairs nod in the spring weather, reminding me of the porch of the Evangeline Inn, in Wolfville, Nova Scotia, where the faces were not Chinese, but as inscrutable. Speak to me not of Anglo-Saxons and the middle class, for there I, unhappily, but increasingly, belong.

First impressions of Sandro: power, impudence (a king can say anything), grace.

> *There are two sisters, one is a rose*
> *And no one knows what the other is.*

Leah: something strange and troubled, at the first re-meeting. A set of Chinese boxes. The princess in the tower, in the thicket, untouchable: first corruption of reality into romanticism. Her mind, in spite of personal pressures (and what is more personal than a sister?), is somewhere else. Inside herself she avoided me, like a woman not wanting to go to bed with her man. Some guilt there. Never was a confider, but still, on that night...

I had a cat once who hated the typewriter and moaned as I punched out the crap that earned my way in the academic. Compared with Leah, he was open and honest. Leah, who is to be remembered eating olives, adding me up. Like H. James, Esq., I am interested in inscrutability, even after Thurber.

After that evening there was no post-mortem. I said to Joe, "You're right, she's lovely," and he held his peace. We dozed in the train to Marseille, where we separated, hung over with events. Anyway, Christmas was not far off.

Then two days later I was upstairs at Aix putting off reading about French West African writers, when Renée the soubrette panted down the corridor to announce a gentleman, one who has made her preen and bob and dart. Probably a representative of the organization which is paying my way: I tidy myself without enthusiasm, pull on a sober look, assume briskness, and find Sandro pacing the *tomettes* of the hall. He has been in Marseille on business; Leah is with a friend in Nice. Shall we spend an afternoon together?

Small talk, to begin with, about African writers, about primitive cultures. I have a not surprising feeling this could turn to phallicism, so we steer toward money: an account of my battles with the landlady about rent. He is shocked at the amount, says he can fix it. But it is not my money it is paid with, she feeds us astonishingly well, she can have it: he calls me very American, very rich, and we laugh.

Still there is an ugly constraint. Comes the moment when we know we do not know each other. In these circumstances it would be better to be walking than driving (he goes too fast over this landscape, like a native) and yet, the way things are now, is walking not too intimate, a shared recreation, not a function like a ride in a car? We go rather silently north, over the uplands and by the châteaux, under liver-marked plane trees under a surly sun. We repeat names which are pleasing to our ears. There is nothing else to say.

For me, he is the classic, legendary male. In profile, the eagle personified: haughty, in his high-bridged nose, dark, but with that tinge of redness which indicates a blond ancestor, and direct. I do not deceive myself that there is not something devious also, he thinks too long before answering questions, half closing his eyes, sucking his cigarette. Not choosing English words, choosing the one possible answer. And in our ready-made intimacy, we pretend that we are being as direct as we could be. "You are diffident," he says. "You are afraid."

"Always afraid of making a fool of myself."

"I find this strange; it is obvious that you know what you think."

"I don't always know how it will be taken."

"You are either a coward or a pessimist."

I thought this clever of him at the time; I am usually taken simply as aggressive.

"In the olden days, Sandro, we called it shy."

"I said to myself when I first saw you, this girl is not being herself."

"Oh, at the dance, it was impossible to be anything but an actress, and I am a bad one. Leah..."

"She is a very good actress."

"Of course."

"But I was more interested in you."

It was a long time since I had had a man's whole attention in that way. The *New Statesman*, Genet, Maeght's gallery—things kept coming between me and men. I squirmed in the limelight, loved it. Ah, but the good men always went early, that was the point of the furbelows of adolescence: training for the capture. While Leah was learning to tame her hair, I was practicing walking over gravel in my bare feet. If I had married Sandro instead of Leah—if I instead of Leah had married Sandro—ah, we should not be talking under the *tour communal* of Manosque, hearing stained sheep, we should be worrying instead over the staleness, over the children. And if, instead of Leah, I had been in my buckram bathing suit on her island at the beach—if he had met me instead of Leah? We should have had one conversation about the difficulty of swimming with a load of books on the chest, I should have learned a lot about dredging and diving, Sandro would have married a rich cousin.

"What are you thinking?"

"Life is a bowl of shit. Sturgeon's Law."

"And what am I?"

"One of the nice little seeds left for birds like me."

He gave me his measuring look, like Leah's, who

had caught it from whom I could not remember, and I thought, they haven't always been engineers, first they were merchants, then they were soldiers. I could see him weighing gold, with his veiled eyes, weighing gold and fingering lace, there was Byzantium in him with all its engineering birds, and Venice, Islam, the Jews.

"My sister is a scholar."

"Ah, yes?"

"She is at the university in the Abruzzi. She is a historian."

"Much better field than English. You shouldn't be able to get to the bottom of it."

"Have you? Is that why you're unhappy?"

"I suppose I've only come to the end of my interest in my subject."

"She is an authority on the period when Ravenna was the capital of Byzantium."

"She must be happy."

"She is a hunchback."

There was not a stock reply, so I let him go on.

"You look as if you wish you were one."

"It would narrow the field."

"You shouldn't have to bother about men."

"I don't know why one does."

"Because one has to, as men bother about women. And I think she is bothered. But in Italy—oh, ugly women have a better time in England."

"Oh, I don't know."

He paused, then nearly shouted me off my chair. "*Mon dieu*, that's it, that's what's strange about you, you think you are ugly. Oh strange, strange sister." He spouted gusts of laughter and ordered more Pernod.

"Look, I have to get back to Aix."

"To stir about in your bowl of shit? I have to go and see a client. Come, *belle laide*, I can't deliver you back yet. Once upon a time there was a princess who thought she was a toad..."

"Look, I really must try to find a bus..."

"Shut up, rat-face..."

"But beside Leah..."

"Beside Leah you are a simpleton and big girl. Now come along, we are going to see a beautiful piece of engineering on the Durance, which is rather far away. We shall drive fast; you are to feel beautiful, so that you can sound very intelligent, and pretend to be my wife. My client is a Protestant."

VI

From another stage in my life, I have a Greek record; a raucous bouzouki band jiggles: *Thalassa, pos me pikranes*, O sea, how much my sorrow... They sing it as if sorrow were some sort of party, and they are probably, as usual, right. Pre-Freudian psychology, the need for catharsis. I turn the record up loud because the man next door is beating his son. I'll welsh to the cops the day I move, not before, the man has been giving me an evil look.

And I was playing it the day my father died, among a web of tubes.

The little cat died too, gave up his rodents and roaches, his moanings, his red flannel catnip mouse, puked green, sat in a draft. The Vet shook his head—hadn't I known about distemper shots? Feelings of loss transferred themselves, I invested this wet fur with all my mourning. It shivered and vomited, lost its gloss. We were alone and destitute, it knew, and as I was forcing glucose down its skeletal jaws, expired.

Thalassa, me pikranes.

I am an old woman now, fingering my books, with talk of leaving. I have seen a man grow old in hospital, I have held twitching, spattered fur. There are things which do not matter any more.

Sometimes, still, I wake moaning for Sandro. The alley sounds like the cobbled passages of his Venice. Some radio brings the distant music of the opera. There is a girl around the corner who looks like the oily little stripper from Martini's. On rainy days I sit reading *Time* in the Honey Dew at Carlton and Yonge and pretend it is Florian's, a caricature of something. Here are Rotarians quick-lunching; bums, Swedenborgians, queers, men mumbling about Castro, all driven from the park. But in Florian's there are mirrors and panels, it is Mitteleuropa with a hazy Italian touch, not Toronto. Leah hunches over her chocolate, brooding. I see her and think of running away, for I have come early to Venice, to see it for myself, after Aix turned to ashes. For four days in the damp weather, I skulked its museums, discerning what I could in the absence of electricity; looking, too, for Joe, who must have received my wire. From the hotel in the Rialto, I went every day, sometimes by vaporetto, sometimes over the willow pattern land way, to meet the Paris trains. That Joe should come. Something I did not like was continuing to happen to me, he had to come and once more help. All my training, all my walking on gravel, was slipping away. I knew what I wanted and Joe had to save me from it. But instead of Joe, there was Leah hunched over chocolate, dead-eyed, and it could have been either of us at the station in the form of that rubbery old woman, scarfed and optimistic, who had met every Paris train since 1943. Both of us were, it appeared, always disappointed.

Leah: There you are, you have a telegram. She

showed no sign of surprise, as if she were pathetically used to playing this game.

She wore a novelettish little outfit, something from an imitation of Fitzgerald: a red velvet cap, and a leopard jacket that had the underfed look of all European furs. Not that it was cheap, no, but there was a sad little 1929-theatrical look about her, a pretty parcel, left to wait, and uncomfortable under my eyes, but not talking. Never apologize, never explain. I wished I were Leah.

I ordered coffee and sat across from her, keeping her face before mine to block out my own reflection. It was the year of the Vadim film *No Sun in Venice*. "It's dreary," she said. "Isn't it?"

"Venice?"

"I suppose for you it's wonderful. For me, that's worn off. In the winter I only hope to stay alive."

"I've been trotting about like a madwoman with a guidebook. Enjoying it."

"I know. Sandro saw you in the Merceria."

"Oh."

"He thought it was very funny. It's the sort of thing I do, sneaking around without anyone's being the wiser."

"I got sick of Aix—it's not a good winter town. I was going to stay in Milan but it looked awful."

"You can check out of your hotel and come to us any time."

They lived somewhere on the Zattere, near Ruskin's plaque, but I had not spied out the exact building.

"I hope you live in a palazzo."

"God, no. We're in a modern flat. We're not rich, you know."

"The family?"

"They have one, but there's nothing aristocratic about them, you poor romantic. They're a mixture of Austrian, Greek, English, Jewish and *petit commerçant*. They must have bought their surname, though my mother-in-law has a long story about the Venetian empire."

"I know, I've looked them up."

"They're pretty terrible people." She said this with warmth and acidity, indicating that she had been through all the stages of in-law appreciation.

"So you hate Venice now?"

"Not really." She brushed the question off. "It's only—the winter's damp and dreadful. And I was waiting for someone who didn't come."

I wondered if I had driven him away.

We paid and left together. That night I left the hotel for the Zattere. The building was modern, and I had to shout my name five times through an intercom before the maid buzzed the door open. I left my suitcase in the lobby and ran up four flights of stone stairs for Joe's telegram. He wasn't, of course, coming.

Leah's sons are sturdy, blond, and affectionate. Multilingual. As soon as I saw them I started wanting Antonio.

Ach, Antonio, your almost-mother is a fool. Anne of Green Gables reaching above her station, turned bum. Up my street all day wander the dispossessed and because my country is a northern one the dispossessed are the sodden. On the radio there are forums to discuss the causes of dispossession, to distinguish between the chicken and the omelette. Though before I rented this apartment I did not know what company I was to keep, I have known since I was born that here, I belong among the one-legged, sodden, wrong-colored, prompt-at-the-hostel. In the park they are all religious maniacs, and Nazis, preaching on Sunday, and throwing stones. They come to preach to us, but we are indifferent. With considerable passion I espouse my neighbors, and because of this affinity, O would-be child who could not grow up to be his mother, after the visit to Barbados and Sandro, I went to Montreal and had you, like my tonsils, out.

Two years have confirmed my stubborn optimism, I still want my Antonio. He would have been like Sandro—another reason for squelching him—he would be strong to smile, and loving and—oh, unborn. I wanted someone to share the sadness of what I know. I wanted someone to show the world to. I wanted my Antonio. I still want him.

Sometimes, I tell myself, I am saving up for him, he and I will grow up on some island together, like Durrell and his perpetual girl infant under the olives, serious but carefree. I want him to be a dark, knowing little boy, big-boned and gracious. This male image of myself would comfort me, give me a shred of the future. But what would I give him?

Here and now the fizzed Chinawoman next door is brooming three bums out of the booze can. The cops come to zip their flies, frisk them, stack them in a blue chauffeur-driven Studebaker Lark. One Indian, two Saxons, lolling. Could see them lying masturbat-

ing on the floor until one vomited; then, out: evacuate
your methyl alcohol in a cell, this is Toronto.

No place for Antonio.

Of course I could have had him and given him
away. That's popular. With impotence rising, young
Wasps are desperate to litter. I could fill a suburban
cradle with a specimen, any color I want but Indian.
Only the spastic, the half-possessed you can't give
away. It's one way of dealing with morality.

But poor Antonio went into a basin after the universal mechanical screw. Me retching yellow mor-
phine. What's the better part?

There has to be a certain kind of world, where
people are admitted. Antonio, I say, Antonio I say feebly as the hormones mount, will live where it is admitted, only where it is admitted that man is a domesti-
cated carnivore who has canted his nature to suit his
convenience. Say that here, you're in the loony bin.
This town's a tea party, no room, no room.

Venice? The streets are cobbled, there are no cars.
The motorboats are sinking the palazzos, when the Ca'
d'Oro dies we'll mourn out our lives. The beef is veal,
but next to the CNR switching yards in Galt, the only
pure heaven is the fish market. Every alley would be
exalted with Antonio. Though Alex and Lorenzo go
nowhere without their nanny, my Antonio would run
free and shouting like the kids who soar round the corner shouting "That whole wide wooooooorld." Look at
me, everything was ordered and organized: nothing.

When I left Venice after the new year, I wanted
instead to take a room in the Ghetto so Sandro could
come and beat me once a week. My life was simplified

and refined. Nothing had happened yet, though he was beginning to be irritable, irritable and restless. Because my sister, that princess in the distant tower, had had enough of holidays, and was obviously anxious to return to her waiting post at Florian's? I was impatient for Joe, as if I didn't know my life raft was occupied. And I had to go and tell him how he had caused me to lose my life in some way I was too lazy to understand.

By this time Leah and Sandro had put their town through its paces for me. Venice put on a flood, and filled the piazza: the populations of Padua, Mantua, Verona, and Ravenna turned up in rubber boots to paddle. Florian's looked disapproving. Normal errands were rerouted through the Merceria, where the shop windows were fitted out with goods the colors of rubies and emeralds, without benefit of Santa Claus. Swamped gondolas lay at mooring posts, subsiding with their own romantic humors. Sunset was not Turner's gold, but powder box colors which no sophisticate would admit, and glowing. Pink, in fact, and blue, with clouds. Soon after, Venice put on snow. In Florian's, we felt muffled against the velvet. We persuaded Sandro to take us to Harry's Bar, even though he disapproved: there was something exciting which he could not understand about going through swinging doors from the vaporetto stop. Once, a lone tourist in the stone-cold palace of the Doge, I heard steps behind me, ran over the Bridge of Sighs without looking out, panted past dungeons. He caught me, laughing. There was almost an embrace.

The family Bragadino occupied one floor of a palazzo locked in some dark quarter I could never find again. At the Christmas gathering there was a schism between the sophisticates and the enjoyers, as there is when city people at home indulge in a country Thanksgiving. Fat aunts were pasta-scented, thin aunts fashionable: only Sandro bridged the gap. He, of his generation, was the only man, the king. His mother's side, proper, savagely girdled, and glaring, vied in cosseting him with his paternal aunts, the fat ones, one of whom actually sold crystallized fruit. His hunchbacked ·sister, home from the Abruzzi, was entirely silent. She looked sharp and self-absorbed. With Leah and the children she got on well, but one glance in my direction froze her attention away. I knew what she was thinking, was glad she was unaware of (or was she?) the hollowness of my degree. But her ugliness, had she known it, was an asset, part of the decadent splendor of the city. Caterina in her palazzo, Leah in leopard waiting at Florian's, Sandro indignant at the existence of Harry's Bar, steps in the dungeon behind me: conjunctions to be regretted, and run away from.

"I think," he said at the station, "that you are rather running away from me."

You bet I am. "No, I have to go to London."

"That is ridiculous. You could spend the winter here. Leah would be happy with such company."

At that I knew he was a liar. "Thanks, but I have a thesis meeting, and courses to prepare for next year."

"At any rate, we shall see you before you leave Europe."

"In the spring, probably. I'm thinking of going to the Greek islands."

"No, spend the summer with us. We have an island..."

Listen, I've got all the romantic diseases, islands included. Lay off.

But he did not. He reached into the reticule containing my personal icons. Now I have no Antonio, no Joe, no Sandro, no Father, no cat.

VII

Pa left me a few things. Shields. Organs, African violets, John Strange Winter, and the truss store. Also, of course, my system and my constitution.

These are the things that made me, articles from the world of celluloid and composition (for which give me polyhexamethyleneadipamide any day) and the bonesetter. The man who made a fortune in the rayon and rubber lecherousness of shields has of course died horribly. These were handed to one, like the razor for the armpits, at thirteen, so that hairless, odorless Porlocks, whose arches were supported by Oxfords, with purged systems and excellent constitutions, could be sent out to tend their African violets with Royal Purple Pot Pills after having their advice about drinking from a yellow-bound volume called *A Name to Conjure With* by John Strange Winter, a great hairy woman, dark and flesh-tongued as the goddam violets, the real cause of shields and razors. She looked as if she needed a truss, and her book was diarrhea colored, stamped in green.

There was this woman who was a good wife, whose houseplants never died, whose children had blond curly hair, and whose only problem was that she married a Weakling. Weak in the lungs, the inheritance, and the earning power, he had more and more to rely on his resourceful wife's literary leanings, because they couldn't pay the maid to press Fauntleroy's frills or the nanny to curl Eva's hair without Mother's industrious scribblings. Father got weaker and weaker, but the scribbling paid off, there were best sellers and parties, and pressure from publishers, and no doubt attentions to be paid to the William Morris wallpaper. Nothing gained without effort has value, however: in order to produce siblings to the best-sellers, our heroine has to work nights after an exhausting day in the African violet factory (mending the children's trusses), the pressure begins to exhaust her, and to sustain herself she takes to draughts of a little something.

A green liquid; it writes marvelous books and it is alcoholic.

Odd, the only drink my mother ever wanted to try was crème de menthe.

For four hundred pages, our heroine dashes off three-volume romances, cossets husband and children, sees to the upholstery, and plunges every night into the little green bottle. What more could a woman want?

Shields? Absinthe probably makes her stink. It also ruins her disposition, runs up the liquor bill, shows her what a clot her husband is, and makes her conscious that her children are ninnies. So she goes out into a church in a square and meets this priest, see, and he says...

Well, I don't suppose very many children read the book when I did, and nobody surely has since, but lady,

I wouldn't give it to your daughter, it will corrupt her as surely as it did me. Because the priest tells the heroine to give up writing, and she does. In the end they are happily settled in a humble cottage; she is doing her own housework, her husband has some kind of occupational therapy and Fauntleroy has his hair cut. The empties have presumably been sold at a profit: fade out into the Church Commissioners' slums in Paddington.

Now when I was ten I knew better than that, even if under Sunday School pressure I signed the pledge at twelve. The first drink I had, at twenty-one, was blackberry brandy, and since the trap door to hell did not open and the stuff did not induce me to write a masterpiece I became neither a great writer nor an alcoholic. But I love my booze as well as most of the bums on this street, and if you asked me to choose between books and booze vs. home and William Morris wallpaper I wouldn't have to think. I was corrupted early. Morality plays always backfire.

Ah well, now we have a metabolism to be vague about, and it's propped up with a pig's kidney at that.

We're heading for the moon without knowing we grew up on it.

Mother was forty when Leah and I were labored into her world; a minister's daughter, born before Victoria died. Peg and Rosemary were six and eight; the family lived in a world that was as personal and physical as a Victorian parlor. The culture gap had not shut far enough to let Canada be in any way "modern" without guilt, and we were farther from the present than most of our friends, the majority of whom were raised with Shirley Temple dolls, tap-dancing lessons, and ringlets. We envied the poor up-to-date beggars sent into snowdrifts in cute little knee socks, unaware of the buckle galoshes, darned lisle stockings, surgical Oxfords that created a bond between Porlocks and the few other victims of home and healthy traditions. It is, in fact, Henry Miller's turn-of-the-century childhood I share more than my contemporaries', the breathy snug shabbiness of the bad old days dying late and hard, togetherness on a piano bench with fat music teachers who smell of hair oil; we had antimacassars and because the King had only five inches of water in his bath, we were washed down in a tepid iron sink; our house had a real English scullery and a real English chill. Flannel bloomers, cotton waists, boys in breeks, and a perverse aura of sex in everything: smut, and the aromatic unknown, and all the words for it Anglo-Saxon and onomatopoeic.

Auntie Vi who lived with us a while "never matured," the whisper-hiss said; the music teacher Miss Osborne was "having the change of life" and cried when our Hanon exercises went wrong. They had the same flesh both of them, powdered with the smell of peppermint over perspiration. The undersides of their hands were fatty as frogs', they were as unspecifically obscene as altered toms and four-letter unknown words on United Church walls. If that was sugar and spice.

Sandro on a business trip to London (where he looked wrong) tried to place the difference between me and Leah. "Leah," I said, "never had a love-hate relationship with her mother's flesh-colored corset strings." She had, in fact, quietly from the beginning of her life, and tidily, rejected the significance of everything I found bearable in our existence. She squatted in corners telling herself stories, to be far away from us. No snugness of armpits for her, no glorying in repellent love. I ooze, booze, stink, feel human rather than feminine, live in a welter of Kleenex and newspapers, cats, clay pots, pictures of people, dust. She is cool as a cat, aware, and apart.

Sandro swears that he is sociologically fascinated. I am relieved that that is all, because I have a committee meeting at two and I can't for want of wardrobe go to The Establishment and there's the ball to get rolling for the American visa. I dismiss him.

But not without cutting my throat.

I shall have four months free before my return to North America; I have an atlas, with maps of islands. I consult him on the location of paradise.

When I am at last rebaptized Dr. Porlock I am empty and pale. By selling books and an insurance policy I limp across Europe, feeling as real as the nets of mistletoe in the greening trees, to my further island. Because after this I shall be a confirmed and inevitable academic, and everything will change, I take the last of my innocence further abroad.

The island is flat, warm, empty as I am. Here I can rent a peasant's house, buy local cloth, have sandals made, clothe myself in arty indigence. I have a pile of notebooks, some novels which I never open, and a trampled mind. It is as close to the Levant as I have been, I am as close to a vegetable as I have been. I get up at dawn, swim, eat, sleep, and repeat the cycle until another dawn. England begins to ooze out of me as the rocks heat in the sun. I brown slowly, play Robinson Crusoe. I know it cannot last as an experience, so I savor it. I could not be more dead if for the past four years I had slept with a stake through my heart at Charing Cross. This is the revival, the beginning of a seepage of reality, here where people eat, sleep, breed, fight, all with exaggeration and charm— oh it's hell going round making goo-goo eyes at the Merrie Peasants, it's arch and out-of-date, but after London, four years up to the ears in grit, after châteaux and *hotels particuliers* and palazzos and *appartements de grand standing*, to see an old woman in a spotted kerchief hoeing beans, wiping her grandchild's snotty nose, carrying a basket of fish, to see these tanned and tattered and unself-conscious men hauling in their boats, or sprawled in the village café—it's a purge. Condescending to watch and live among them, one never achieves even the status of the "summer people" in villages in Canada. But there's air. And they would go to the cities to gawk if you offered them a chance. So I went to look at the human carbon chain, intimately connected with their functions and their futures, balm for isolation.

But after a fortnight I was conscious of shadow over me, looked up to see Sandro. "So here you are," he said.

"Where's Leah?"

"Oh, she has gone to Paris with my sister. Tell me how you live here."

"Still collecting notes on relations?"

"No, having a holiday with you."

Don't ask how it is done, just do it.

VIII

Fables and sonnets, Sarah falling into little flowers as she walks beside him. Aroynt thee, witch, but no: "Here is an island. It is a good island, with young mountains, dry plains and wet plains, mountain villages, seaside villages. Little white houses and a warm climate. In summer it is very hot and you lose your temper. Now it is very nice.

"On this island grow lemons, oranges, aubergines, vines, and sheep with fat tails. Everything globular, because the houses are square. The people drink a lot of wine.

"I am a tall, dark man. I have a blue English car. I sit in the car beside a tall Woman with brown hair. Her face is wide and amusing, she has large, kind hands. I want to make her touch me with her hands, but I am also quite an old man, so I drive my car.

"I drive my car first down the streets of an old town, where the people take their siesta in front of their shops and workrooms. There where they tan sheepskins the road stinks. Across the road a fat man is hammering out a copper boiler. He makes a fine noise. They are honest, working people here. We are on a holiday."

His primer of the history of desire.

"Now, Sarah, below us is the mother sea. Once we were in it, little bits of jelly, before we were aphids or apes or knights and ladies. And it will not be long, Sarah, before there are no more knights and ladies.

"Today the mother sea is very blue. It is warm as urine. You and I wear light clothing, and in the car we have our bathing costumes, and several bottles of the dark red liquid, wine. We shall find a road over the mountains, on the other shore, where we can hunt wild plants, pretend we are seals in cold water, and drink our wine.

"See, Sarah, down through the lemon trees is the sea. It is real and salt. Today you are going to meet it, and reality, which is acts with names, things with definitions, and putting acts and definitions and names and objects in order. Because I am the man I am, I cannot allow you to waver. But I do not think the truth will set you free.

"See, Sarah, there are mountains, and in the mountains, though they are rather low, and young as mountains go, but steep, there are fortresses and castles. They were built by soldiers and slaves many many years ago, when the soldiers built and killed in the name of God. And when they built those castles they had many quarrels, both with their enemies and with their own bodies.

"Even in those days marriage had been invented, although it was not at all like marriage now because the ladies had to do what their fathers and husbands told them, and they were only allowed to be married to one person. But like all of us they wanted more than one, for one person cannot be perfect enough.

"I am not perfect, you are not perfect; we may dream of being perfect together and making perfect children, but if I live close to you for ten years I shall develop such a hunger for perfection that I shall go mad and think I can achieve this with quite another person—especially with one with whom I am not obliged to live. Those who do not care about perfection escape this madness, of course, but they are very dull.

"Look, Sarah, look at the castle. I have been here before, I know this island well. I know there are caper flowers blooming in the castle, and all the people are gone. Let us stop the car and look at the castle.

"I pee, Sarah pees. Sarah's shoes are full of dry earth. Sarah does not quite approve until I say, 'It was a good pee.' Then Sarah laughs. See, that Sarah laughs. In my car, two people laugh. The man who drives takes the lady's hand. She coughs.

"Look, Sarah, in the periscope of your mind at the people. This is a man with a woman. The woman is afraid, she is red in her face, and she is touching the hand of the husband of her sister, and it is a long way up the mountain to the castle. The lady's sister is far away, Sarah, and so are her mother, her father, and her lover. Remember that it is not enough to have everything around you beautiful, remember that there must also be change and flux, because it is through change that we pretend that we can make decisions, and keep our pride, and go on pretending that both change and choice exist.

"Now we have found a place by the sea. There are stones, but no bathers. See, Sarah, there is a cave. A cave is a hole in a rock, sometimes containing sheep, sometimes anchorites. See, Sarah, see the anchorite's cave, look into your head and see the holy madman and ask what reality he lives with.

"Touch the sea, Sarah. It is wet. Both of us came from the sea.

"You are tall, Sarah, walk over the stones. Look at the sea and the cave and the sun. Let the sea rise on you, Sarah, and lap you. Do you think Aphrodite had such a Canadian face? Do you say I speak as I do because of the wine? Run, Sarah, run.

"You and I are king, Sarah, climb the waves and the world is wide. Egg and dart, spoon and bird, come back, come back, come back."

Once when another aunt was staying with us, who was all lace and coolness, and, Ma said, selfish, once I went into the bathroom and in an ecstasy of devotion rammed my toothbrush into the case with hers. They had to operate.

If I had my Antonio I would go and live in a cave with him and teach him all the rhymes and all the ways of being.

An arrogance was stamped upon me, I changed, though he said I could not. There are no other men who are like him. No one else makes me think of the dark room in the Ghetto where he would beat me once a week. I am arrogant and stupid and think that only that would suit.

Last night three leather hoods picked up one of the tarts down the street, raped, beat, and killed her.

It is almost a relief to believe in evil again, knowing at last that for some things there is no excuse.

He said to me somewhere along the road when my perceptions were still frozen with fear and gratification, he said, "You know, Sarah, you could be something, something sensational. I feel as if I could change your life."

I think he had something like a good haircut in mind, but the effect was different: I had to make room in my conscience for error. I began immediately to be translated from him, and raging Sarah was born.

I liked the little cat's malevolence, which all went out of him when he sickened: the real reduction. He became grateful, too human. In people I also prefer the animal side, it's easier to forgive.

Well, hitch a donkey to a prayer wheel, slap the cards down fast, one after another, play all day, do the rhythmic things, ride the waves, keep up with the dance, and you'll hear some of the music of the spheres they raise you to listen for. But remember, if it's electronic, God is a cathode, and it's all your own fault.

Ah jeeze, they sit up there in their big houses, shooting off their mouths, get a chesterfield, stop smoking, eat regular, Sarah, go to church, stay away from the liquor store, have kids, meet me for lunch at twelve, live a godly and sober life, only we're not Anglicans so don't get poetic about it, persevere, keep your socks up, clean your fingernails, stop picking your nose, wear shoes, stop thinking and snuggle up to God.

They come pouring out of the wealthy suburbs, their machine guns loaded with roses. I feel them descending; the thought of the Parkway is heavy with them, the seed of the ancestors, descending.

The street is too small for them, they disperse and come at me from behind the Welfare, the Victorian Order of Nurses, the E. Fry Society, the Provincial Police. I see them coming in grey felt and fur, I watch them, defenseless at the window. "Cover your breasts," Joe shouts. "They're coming." And he not able to find his address book.

I have a sword. An English, not a Roman one. Could I be noble? I'll get my chance.

They gust through the house, carry me away with them, but they can't see him. When they have Auschwitz in mind they can't see anyone but me.

Pa figured, if he couldn't give us money, he'd give us ambition; he sat heavy after work on the brown fuzz chesterfield, explaining how we could be something. Just not to bury your talent. Just become the best. Work more than anyone else.

Poor Pa, he never knew, never had a chance to find out. Something in him was turned off or never turned on. He never knew what too big a dream could do, and how if you're going to make big dreams in other people, you have to stuff content in. Like the American people, getting bigger every day and not any better, the Porlocks were pregnant with dreams and spawned tadpoles. Of what we wanted to be, we are all the most. Of what we might be, nothing.

And we'll all die of cancer with the rest.

I like the bums down here, vandals and scandals, rapists, robbers, nothings, unfortunates, though just try to introduce me to one and I'll tell you about theory and practice. I like to watch them with their outward and visible signs of an inward and invisible misery. A woman in blue protrudes down the street. She's one. Shall I join her? No, middle class I was born...

At one stage I wanted to be a belly dancer. Much later I saw them in Athens, and thought about the exercises. At fifty I'll be teaching ninth grade English at Peterbell or Listowel and they'll say, that poor old maid.

Brush your teeth, clothe yourself, go out into the world and make stools of ambition. On bleached lawns and in box houses, there are organized, emasculated children, gutless, maleducated; vandals of telephone booths because they cannot be vandals of untruth. Rosie wants peace for her children, not logic. Get up, brush the predigested cornflakes off your predigested gums, clean the smog out of your livingbox, suck the muck from the chemical carpet and breed for the sake of your prosperous, irradiated, ruined, and dog-eared country. To do my best to do my duty to God and the King:

Lovelace, I have quite lost my wits. But I will not except my life.

"Kid," he said, "that's the only little pussy you've got and the only little pussy you'll ever get, go wash it."

"Get on with you, Sally," says Desmond the Reilly, "it's all wind in the chimney, what you're saying. What's so wrong with it, this country and this world? Your sisters are living like nice happy girls with happy little kids and husbands. It won't hurt their kids not to do logic in school. They don't love their fellow men all they could, but they love him more than you do. Relax and enjoy life now, instead of repeating vile stories. Get married, have a babba or two, stop worrying, and just be the nice, well-built woman you are."

The club is sooty with dark. The devil's advocate parts his hair in the middle. His brogue is his Sunday best. I shouldn't have screamed out at him, pity to upset him, they don't like me much here any more, but I have to wail that it might keep going on.

"Live on, Sally," he says. "Don't give a damn. You've a fine big bust and a fine confused mind. You can cook, don't turn out to be one of them spoilers. Enjoy your life for the dear Lord's sake, you've done quite a lot with your life for a woman, and don't sit saying you can't do more because you're not a big Eye-tie with a French education. You're a nice Canadian girl with long legs and enough behind to make bedsprings worthwhile, if we didn't drink so much of this here rotgut Canadian rye whisky we'd do something about it."

Enter Eldon, who chooses not to see me. Desmond muzzles me. "You're only making trouble, now, I think I'll take you home. I'll put you to bed and you can practice some of your sad total recall on me. I suppose you've even forgotten to feed that cat. Oh, he's dead, is he, God rest him? Here, Orestes, put it all on my bill, I'm taking her ladyship home before she bites her brother-in-law."

Desmond only sticks me because he hopes Eldon will get him on television, and knows now it's a loser's game. Still, his wife goes to bed at half past nine, and he likes to talk.

"If you'd only unclog," he complains, "you could go on the air yourself. You ought to be good at quizzes and such, and we could curl your hair and tart you up a bit. You know semibeatniks like you are right in style now, in a year you'd be making a fortune which I of course as impresario would be pleased to share. But you want it all both ways, don't you? Well, perhaps you're right. Got your key? Why don't you go and be sick and come back to old Des cheerful?"

Not to throw stones, I pretend to go and be sick. But I'm almost sober, it's just natural obstreperousness tonight, not wanting to hate Desmond and his Keep Going Half Truths, which he keeps in his Irish waistcoat, nostrums against despair. It's all very well for him to keep going, he's being grand though I hear he's lost all his money again, but what I need is more Stop And Look Fortifying Pills. Funny old Desmond, he's the kind of optimist who can't see that even if the sun's shining the wind might be bad for your sinus. I'm the reverse, out on a limb now, too, with the tree crunching behind me. What Des won't believe is that the world, like Desmond, is a charming deceiver, calling "Go on, go on..." until someone is teased to challenge it and stop. Think, kiddies, your lollipop is poisoned, your mattress is an Uglirest, and the concepts upon which you are being fed are—hilarious. What you have to do is stop being brave and plodding, look around.

"Eldon doesn't look well at all," Desmond complains.

"I've been hexing him lately."

"Sarah, you're unkind."

"In my small way, Des, I like to try to improve the world. They give him half an hour's television time every week to explain his philosophy of death. During that half hour I concentrate on undermining him. It's my Christian duty."

"And what if you make your poor, sick sister unhappy?"

"Happiness is not necessarily a good thing. She'd work more without him."

"And then why do you sit and wail in the club about your own unhappiness until I have to mop you up and transport you home?"

"For the pleasure of the mop, I expect."

"Well, if you'll tell me where you keep the kettle, I'll put you on some tea. If I were older and closer to heaven, or younger, or closer to sin, I'd see if I could put a grin on your feminist mug. But the truth is, I suspect you wear a vest, and I haven't the courage to find out. You think you're persecuted, but you're a form of a persecution yourself."

"If you came to thinking my way, Des, we could clean the lot of them up."

"Ah, my way's better, get yourself a hundred thousand a year and laugh your ass off at them."

"Go home and screw your wife and make another baby before the mutants take over."

"Saving your reverence, I will."

IX

Sandro liked meat: domestic, game. Meat and a variety of meat. Thrushes stuffed with truffles, beefsteak, skewered robins, fat salmon, sucking pig, plump guinea fowl. Women became succulent before him. I could see him before his harem, his black eyes weighing and choosing. I could see him as that African chieftain who fattened his wives until they could only wallow like seals. He liked meat, but he did not like women. He treated them well, but he treated them, handled them: always failed to admit them as equals. Thus at the edges of his behavior were arrogance, contempt, and a fringe of fear.

I, obedient child of how many years? Twenty-five, I suppose, I hate to count. I was respectful before him. Since he was not of my world I did what he said; abdicated my education and was commanded. For a while he found this attitude pungent; but a summer squall arrived and we declined into talk.

"Tell me about marriage," I said, as if it were a strange new thing, as if his primer were a real beginning for me.

In the beginning... I made him begin there, at the point where his oil-prospecting rig was tied up at

Midland because someone had petitioned against pollution of the lake; pending a government hearing, Sandro and his crew were idle. They cruised with their diving gear around the peninsula, and, looking for the Canadian equivalent of amphorae, found our Leah.

It was lyrical, he said, all the epithalamia in literature and heaven, suddenly owning, in the bland, smooth summer weather, my Viking sister, who dreamed at their Italian prow. Even after the collecting of clothing and passports, the arrangement of the marriage at the Consulate, he went on living in a poem and a song. He had several jobs that summer, Bragadino's was trying to expand into the United States, and after they were booted out of the lakes they went to New York, Boston, Gloucester; and with the fine weather, farther south, until with his crew and his new blond specimen, he was called, in the spring, home from the delicious Caribbean, back to injecting Venetian piles with cement.

Until then, there was no worry, no reality. He had sworn before he left Venice to have all the black meat in the world when he went to the Caribbean, but there, with Leah, he forgot. She was a mermaid, a siren, and serene with it. She had something, he said, a sureness that was at the same time vague; he never learned how to read her, she was perpetual fascination. It was a pity that the business was only a business, that they could not stay.

She told me too, about how this time was all gold, and clear, blue water. What it was like to be in love. When the real work was going on, and there was more of it than he admitted, he was an eagle of concentration.

She stayed ashore, tending her fingernails, keeping the sun in her hair. When he came back she took his tension away from him, he buried himself in her and was fresh to begin again. Otherwise, she went out with him, they made love with their masks and fins on...

She did not know what to expect of Venice, there was only a song from school, a lecture or two on Ruskin, Sandro's comparison of the lake with the islands and lagoons. She did not want to spoil the new life by imagining it; she went to Venice as Leah, stood, *tabula rasa* before it; take me as I am.

She was maintained briefly by his stagecraft. He created a grand occasion of the meeting between his city and his wife. They approached by water; no one overwhelming met them. From the ship they were taken into the gondola of an old friend. She floated, then, under bridges by palazzos, on a cool spring morning, into his shimmering city.

His friend prepared carefully her entry into the bourgeoisie. The wife was French and exacting. She taught Leah a little correct Italian, supervised the acquisition of a very correct wardrobe, introduced her to the patterns her life would follow. So that when she met the proud, polyglot tribe he came from, she knew how to act the acceptable part.

But he had committed a heresy in bringing her, a lovely but undistinguished member of an undistinguished family, without a dowry, and from a country they considered uncivilized. So that although she was oiled and eased carefully into the tight socket of her married life, although they could not fail to approve of her when she gave birth, with difficulty and stoicism, to two sons in two years, the family could not bring itself to accept her.

If she had been a European, they might well have moved into the rickety palazzo; but she was adept in maintaining a foreign isolation, the family were as intimidated as they were hostile. Already, she had had to give in to accepting a maid who reported every gesture they made to her mother-in-law, and a nurse who was horrified by the recommendations of Doctor Spock. They moved from apartment to apartment, after many gloomy consultations on cohabitation. Finally, they found the place on the Zattere, which was sufficiently exposed to keep the mother-in-law home nursing her Byzantine sinuses in the winter. They achieved some sort of freedom, but at a cost.

It was more than either of them expected. The margin of profit the firm made was not great, and the Bragadinos, Sandro included, were bent on a fortune. He was, furthermore, keeping her in some style, though she did not realize it. Everyone but the poor friend and his French wife lived this way; she did not know how to make Italian economies, and he did not want her to. Like his cousins, she went to Paris for her clothes when she did not go to Rome or Florence. She took for granted a winter holiday on skis, an island summer. But to support a life on this scale, the firm had to go farther and farther away in the good weather; because of the children, because of the attitude of the family, it was impossible for her to go far with him. And, even in winter, he worked late, came home snappish. Everyone she knew was European, the people were not the gentle people, not the quiet, fussy ones she had known at home. She began to be easily angered and bored. She contemplated having another child, just to garner one more week of fanatic devotion, found herself unable. There were fissures and separations in the idyl. Maintaining her distance from his people took all her moral energy; and it was too hard for her to build a carapace against his people and leave an opening for him. "I should," he said, "have kept her in one of the villages of the lagoon, among the simple people." But he was of his own however provincial metropolis, could only condescend to villages. So she stayed in her tower, and the distance grew.

"Oh, you know," she said to me, "you can grow bored with anyone, even Sandro. And with him it is business, business. Even when we go to Paris, everything is going to be nice, and then someone calls him on the telephone, there is a conversation in numbers and he goes away. I am lucky that I don't get tired of the Louvre, I am certainly not like some women, always buying things."

I wonder if they have any intellectual life to stitch their minds together? Oh, they have been collecting Venetian curios, and antiquities he finds in the Mediterranean, which she studies with his sister, or documents in museums. They wish they had the time, the passion, to know more.

Up to this time he had still not become critically unfaithful. There had been incidents in his long absences, but nothing—personal. Once, however, on a return, he heard words he could not believe. He questioned her, found her involved, whether physically or not she would not tell, with an English archeologist, whom he had removed to another posting at once. It was not three months before she fell pitiably in love with another Englishman. It was always Englishmen, very shy Englishmen, a rejection of his dark forcefulness. He was too civilized to beat her, he would certainly not divorce her; but after that they went their own separate ways.

"You need ties," I told him. "You need to stay close to each other." But who ever got close to our Leah? Shy Englishmen, perhaps.

Well, he said, perhaps I was a tie. Perhaps through me he might somehow tie her down. "Tell me about her," he pleaded.

All those sisters, and none of them I know well. From our childhood I remember principally hostilities, competition, Leah giving me her green, superior look when I burble to Mother that today I'm in love with X. "You only love books," she said, with scorn, which was true, and hurt. So, I told on her, oh, something, she never did what she was told, it was easy to fault her, and the war, begun when I was born, would go on. She got on best with Peg, who was the other quiet one; she always went out with the sleekest, most handsome boys; she kept a diary so well hidden even I could never root it out; she looked after her hair and body and clothes as if they were objects outside her, something you could love, like a thing you were writing, or a precious set of notes. We were scornful of each other, but what hurt me most was that she never envied me.

"She does, you know," he said.

"How could she?"

"I think we all do, now. You have your freedom."

It was a bitter freedom and he was invading it for her sake as I was relinquishing it in order to be her.

"You know," he said (he always began, you know), "from now on I think you will have a great many lovers."

The thought repelled me. One flagrant aberration at a time sufficed. "Why?"

"Because those of us who marry girls who are really good when they're twenty find ourselves at thirty looking for women like you. Women with ideas, interests, minds."

"You're a bunch of Pygmalions, then; little, pretty girls of twenty could become something other than empty-minded mothers at thirty. You have the power to change your wives: you should make them into something you can love."

"We also have to earn their living; there's not time."

"You ought to learn to live a different way. You Europeans always say we live by magazine ads, influenced by a completely artificial norm. Well, so do you. You take a girl like Leah and make her into a little society flower with two beautiful children, so she's just a pretty picture; then you throw her away. Oh, it happens not just here: all over the world."

"There is fault on both sides."

"No doubt."

I thought it would be easier to see him go because we had reached the stage of becoming symbols for each other; but my flesh tore.

The sea and the sun and the sand and the surf, earth, sea, and sky; moon, june; sex. Land of myth, not what I became my own Pygmalion for, nothing to do with selling column inches to the *Temperance Advocate* or licking the windowpanes of the truss store. Copulation might have been in my books, and romance, but not this. I made out the fifteen-year plan when I was too young, ignorant of this tearing feeling, which made a unity of those elements we were carefully taught to separate, so that my albeit now residual intelligence, my dreaming, and my body entered a period of dogged, wrong devotion, over which I had no control.

So also, Joe, with Ruth.

Before, when Joe and I were clever and academic, our most searing experiences had been a sort of *coitus interruptus* by ideas. Sexual activity inflamed our brains, we lost interest at the orgasm, forgot to experience it; especially using each other. A little discipline, the books said, can heal this. We, with our experience of books (the Proust kick, the Thos. Wolfe kick, the Freud kick, the Sartre kick, and what you are doing *there?*), thought that a trip down a darker channel would improve us. Hence Ruth, Sandro.

Joe went back to Paris after the reunion of Porlocks, pleased with himself. He had found both Leah and me lacking; he was freed of us and decided it was time to leave us alone; not without taking note of Sandro. He visualized, with satisfaction, our humping in the hills, before it happened.

Personal myth put away, what next? Wife. Ruth. How can you think in bed with a girl like Ruth? She's always chewing at you; civilized enough, though, anyone who went to a school called Music and Art is civilized (we have this Canadian awe of New York). And she has a talent somewhere. He needs some kind of intelligence and estheticism in his women, but not in bed; no rationalism. From below, she sucks and chews at him, an undernourished sea cow. Out of bed, she is quiet beside him in cafés, but likes speed. Her ideas of marriage are furtive: you sneak away and do it; which they do.

She turns out to be hell in the house, and he finds it matters. She chews gum, they live in what seems to be a comprehensive ashtray. Still, there is money, he has, influenced by new responsibility, managed to send out and sell a handful of articles. Morocco? Listen, she says, let's go home; Canada might be a gas. Someone has offered him a job on the *Star* in Toronto. Hemingway worked there once. Ruth, who is no longer quiet in cafés, decides, let's do it, kid. The café generation in Paris gets ten years younger every three weeks; stone jewelry dies. I was still moodily in Venice when they were preparing their entry into hell.

White shirts, little dinners. Floors to polish. An old grey car which goes very, very fast. She spends his pay on a sewing machine and records. When she is in the mood, they manage to make something of their time. They own a bed, a kettle, and a frying pan, social life requires nothing of them but owning two decent outfits, the crowd on the paper may not be Paris, but they're good drinkers, and good fun. He decides it's a possible place.

She discovers that it is not a gas.

Why did she encourage him to come?

A year later the obvious answer is clear: she is seeking her own destruction and his. He hadn't known about the hypodermic.

It would have been better to return to Europe and lose themselves in the crowd. But there is the fare. And the big seriousness of his old environment is growing in him, he is on a crusade (there are so many things to reform), he is in his country now, he has power to create change. He sees her eyes grow furtive and is too busy to understand. When she meets him in the Metropole she brings the oddest friends, but he rather likes that, her raffishness takes the prosaic edge off high endeavor.

What appalled him was that her slither to destruction was so fast. One day she is laughing with a slouching, earringed youth, the next in jail. He finds himself mirrored in the confession magazines: I married a stranger.

All her stories about herself are untrue. She's a wildcat gone wrong, she's had a record in New York since she was seventeen.

The day he hires a lawyer, he steps into a new world. Detectives find out more about her than he thought it possible to know; they have a malicious interest in tracking down a crusading reporter's wife. In prison, awaiting trial, she is given no assistance with her habit. He becomes a one-man E. Fry Society pleading for help for addicts. He is quizzed on the one side about her friends; on the other about his own resources. And the only help is to have her committed.

He tours the facilities; the city is proudly anti-Freudian and if you lose your mind it's your own fault, faltering among all those churches: a weakness of character. There are no figures on the resuscitation of addicts, he gathers that officialdom considers them a waste of hope. A private clinic is the answer.

When I see him again after earth, sea, sky and humanizing, when I see him, I am trying to get into the Psychiatric to uproot Antonio; and the number of thousands of dollars he is in debt is the gas.

We become an elderly couple, the parents of Ruth. We study her report card, noting hostilities, enumerating weaknesses in the system that made her. Processing the data her subconscious sends the psychiatrist.

Her father is an elderly rabbi in New York who shut his door when she defied him at sixteen. She hates him. He wanted her to shave her head, and for her this is female circumcision: he will rob her of her power to enjoy. But she is guilty, and in her dreams he pursues her. Hound of Heaven? We are not quite sure. Her mother, who has a *hausfrau* complex, she also hates. Her brother is in Israel among the Hassidim: castrated, she says. She has cut herself off from the whole of the Jewish world, which was the only matrix where she felt at home.

Oh, there is more, there is more. But in terms I have not the audacity to understand. She has been hunting for roots, but she hates roots; she is a little textbook of the human race, and there is doubt that she will ever be well.

"It was marvelous," Joe sighs, "for the first while. It was real. We had a few symbolic responsibilities, so that we felt married. Not furniture: a furtive, animal devotion to each other. I knew about the marijuana and was disappointed, even ashamed, that it did nothing for me. I hadn't heard of anyone getting hooked on it, I thought, that's Ruth, part of her, I won't make it go away. I guess I was pleased because I knew she included me in her trances. So we had something I had never had with anyone else.

"But I didn't know about the heroin, any more than I didn't know her father wasn't a professor of fine arts."

Antonio ejected, I took the job at St. A's. I, too, was making a new start, a return to the moral seriousness of my city. I took the slum apartment because it was big and better than ticky-tacky; cleaner, too, before I discovered the roaches. He began to visit at the end of the day; it became pointless for him to go home: because she would be away a long time, because he could not afford his own rent. Each week he added eighty-five dollars to his debt.

Sometimes I caught myself thinking, I am his wife. I enjoyed turning the collars on his shirts. I made him cut his toenails to save his socks, and loved it. He ate breakfast, visited her on time, bicycled to save taxi fares: under my aegis. But I was no sea beast, I could not lose myself any more than he could. I caught him thinking guiltily, this is as good as I can get, and an old friend. We were not obliged to be any better than we were. "Splendidly, that's what we are," he said. "Splendidly null." And stroked me wearily. "What a pity about Sandro, what a fool."

Fool who? I dreamed about him and cried out, disturbing Joe's exhaustion. His two round buttocks were in my dreams and in all the churches. I kept putting my nose to that conditioned grindstone, saying it would go away.

But Sandro made sure it didn't. He wrote, he visited. He picked his moments. I was always in debt to airways and abortionists. I was carrying a more and more terrible guilt. Constantly, my mother quizzed me about Leah, when I saw her last, how she was, as if that girl were her lost child. I forgot her pinched face in Florian's when I heard my mother's fretful voice, I wanted to say "He has big balls." I felt cut off, I couldn't talk to anyone, I was Sisyphus rolling Sandro's balls uphill.

"Sarah has changed," people said, smirking knowledgeably about Yurp.

X

As I said, offensively but without effect, to the journalistic aspirant to the pop-art mind who interviewed me, what I trail behind me is not clouds of glory (he thought Canadians ought all to have bucolic childhoods to fall back on) but memories of my own patterns. Knowing I talk too much, remembering each separate occasion on which I have blethered myself into humiliation, remembering how humiliation made me blether, I continue to talk too much. Hence, after this lotus-position affair with Sandro, I was terrified when my sister Peg married Eldon.

When I first met him there rose in me a fine, pure, instinctive, and personal loathing. If you are allowed to exist, I shouldn't be, my ego said to him, and by God I know which one of us is to be scraped off the earth first. He is what I am told I am, what I am afraid that I am, what I shall kill myself in order not to be (except that I shall not know that I am he until too late): a self-elected personage, a gossip of secondhand values and an impressive range of half-truths. Because, however, I am arts-educated, I can run that love of detail which is presently characteristic of American scholarship against the charge of gossip:

one simply gets into the habit of ferreting out the background. And of course I cannot, though I have tried to, in my own consciousness, change the fact that I am a woman. And my secondhand values are there, though I pretend that they are more carefully culled, better authenticated. Through my cursive readings in psychology (I never read things thoroughly, I am always listening to waves of reaction in my head) I know that behavior tends to repeat itself, I distrust myself when I see him, fear my distaste for him. Incest and identification with Eldon becomes a personal theme, for no old maid's reason.

He shows in his conversation lacunae which are commonly found in the scope of science people and in the self-educated, whose interest in the humanities develops late and after scorn: a tendency to clutch at mysticism, to generalize; a habit of adopting ideas out of context, without evaluation. Even the smattering of philosophy I did not quite listen to could place Eldon in a category to be taken seriously, for he is considered acceptably knowledgeable in the "ogy" of his profession. He was decently trained, he lectures well enough, though like me he is a teacher whom freshmen admire and seniors scorn, knowing they could do as well, more briefly. In his education he was halted by the poor boy's rush to get into the world and help a suffering mother, could not linger in the other faculty's library long enough to form any other attitude but a sneer. His roses must be botanical, his method pristine. When his time came for rumination, his major attitudes were irreversible.

Hence, adolescents are juvenile delinquents, the

poor in situations different from his experience lazy, masturbators, sexual deviates; he would not dare to generalize about his microbes, but confronted by people he shows his old wives' mind and every day I clarify my fear of him.

It is an innocent mind, unable to understand my obsessive appraisal of him. I have to stay sober when I am near him, for if I told him how I felt, he might, because innocent minds are armored against those things they do not clearly perceive, survive; but I should be shattered.

He has become mother, leitmotiv, and demon lover in these last days here. I am surprised that my friends are surprised that I am leaving. No one has said "You're afraid of becoming Eldon."

Sometimes it seems miraculous that even such shadows of intrigue occur in such a town. In manicured neighborhoods, I see people with empty Orphan Annie eyes, and think that only Joe and Ruth and I know that we are alive; that only we know about furtive, furious, internal, and private lives without benefit of IBM machines. There must be thousands of us, because the town has begun to improve, but in the neat north and tidy west, or here in town where reality is shoved fiercely away, where the men cry and reach for their bottles like angry, panicky babies, there is no evidence of an attempt to deal with firsthand truths.

Like "Man is a Carnivore."

The city festers with subcutaneous infection. It was founded by interest and fostered by denial: let not thy left hand...

Ernest Jones came here before the Great War (and by now Ernest Jones should be as important as the Great War) to found a department and preach Freud. He was enthusiastic—"pushy" they must have called him—too much for us. He is remembered as the man who published a paper on Holy Communion as intercourse, and was none too subtly hounded out of town. Now the behaviorists hold us in thrall, and on good nineteenth-century principles Ruth in her private asylum costs Joe every day he owns.

Down here where I live, on a casebook street in the history of urban decay, there are churches as in England there are pubs. There are churches as at main intersections there are banks. Baptist, Presbyterian, United, Anglican, Catholic, Lutheran, Ukrainian United, Free Methodist, African Methodist, Holy Roller, Greek Orthodox, Macedonian Orthodox, Serbian Orthodox, Cypriot Orthodox, Chinese United, Polish Catholic, Deaf, Dumb, Blind, one-footed, half-hearted. The synagogues are farther west.

Churches, and every Sunday they're filled: we sit and hear about sin or the Beatles, the Pope or schism. You'd think after fifty-two Sundays a year for N years we'd know something about our own inner lives.

But no, winos die in the poky, hookers plug C court, magistrates are strict and opaque, Black Marias are full. When the roast is in the oven, the choir sings old, familiar anthems, the good organs hum, hymns comfort the gullet, the pious confess their sins generally or particularly and tisk at the godless about them, while things get worse, not better.

Logic is not taught in our schools. The Ancient

Greeks were not Christians.

Oh, they look after poor motherless babies (having made them by law and persuasion motherless), and they do good deeds, and it's all very nice; only Oz for the first year you're back from somewhere else, and you think, where are the writers, where's the action: how did those painters get there, is there that much admiration of mere work? Where's the wine? Where's the thinking? Oh, it's like Norway, is it, you entertain at home in the winter? Why are they so quiet? Why does one half drug while the other half states firmly that psychological difficulties stem from a lack of will power? Why are there so many Lesbians and dirty bookstores?

More here than meets this eye.

Yesterday, I had lunch with Lyle, that implacably honest, wide-eyed, valuable Dr. Lyle. The woman I should have liked to be, at whom in pressing my views I do not wish to sneer. The woman who gave me what passion for truth I have. I love her, and she makes me squirm.

We had an honest, unpretentious, digestible (but I have the digestion of a goat) lunch at the Toronto Ladies' Club. The sateen environs of.

Now Lyle, I know your reservation about me is that I am flippant. That this is the avoidable defense of shyness. That the Toronto Ladies' Club is convenient, comfortable, and for a women's club... Still, the sateen environs of.

She was as uncomfortable as I. I was sweating. It was like Browning, the last ride together. Love on both sides, good Christian *agape*. I love you but I can no longer go your way, was what I had to say. Exactly like losing one's faith.

It had nothing to do with the fish soufflé, though that was part of the mood. It had, in a way, nothing to do with teaching English. I felt foolish, unformulated, like a freshman ready to shout "I want to burn with a hard, gemlike flame." I knew that although this was a farewell she was giving me a chance to recant, a chance to start again and become what she and I had originally wanted me to be. I think, in fact, that if I had said "Let me teach your Spenser, it will save my soul" she would have unclutched the course. Instead I was tongue-tied. If she talked, there would have been a repetition of the last interview in her office. We were both therefore silent until coffee, awkwardly. She looked stern, watery-eyed, but flustered.

We ordered coffee in the lounge and suddenly broke out in a brandy, which relaxed me. She ordered me another and I tried to open up. But it was hard. Part of the trouble is that communication has come, for me, to have sexual overtones and I don't want to wind up a butch cab driver with a lech for elderly women. And I couldn't say that, so I talked about the other part.

"I have no honest interest in the academic now. I could still be a missionary sort of teacher, but I can't rationalize what I'm teaching. I feel false, phony."

"I have to respect that, Sarah."

"You think these feelings are a luxury?"

"I think they are passing, and masochistic. You need either marriage, or a career. Possibly marriage. Certainly marriage, but you are forgetting that since we cannot all have what we like we must try to like what we have."

"Or rise above the two?"

"I cannot follow you along that line."

"Both alternatives seem to me to be a form of self-indulgence."

"Explain yourself." Her eyes flashed. On the scent, and I loved it.

"The mere idea of marriage is self-indulgence to me; I may need it, I may want it, but the statistical probability of my now finding someone to marry is ridiculous. The only way I shall ever marry is to dismiss the idea, set my heart on something else, and look happy. Still most of the men whom I would naturally, now, get along with, married much earlier women who no longer attract them; so my only hope is a divorced man and a divorced man usually marries his co-respondent. Bachelors of my age are very seldom interested in me. We're single for too many of the same reasons."

"I'm pleased with your reasons: go on."

"The academic comes next."

"I'm feeling rather stronger than you imagine today."

Smile and wince for her understanding. "The academic is simple. There are girls who marry at nineteen to marry... to have the title Mrs. I got my Ph.D. for the same reason. I have absolutely no serious interest in my work that could not be better gratified by teaching high school and I am both too proud and too lazy to do that. And too fond of my own private life. God, I'd have to go to O.C.E. and have some half-assed twirp tell me what to say. So I'd best get out of this country and go to seed. Oh, I'll wind up teaching, or preaching. It's in my bones. But I can't just leave things be."

"Sarah, you know I don't allow swearing to go by without a remark."

"Lyle, you're as full of principles as I am."

"Your generation..."

"You have me confused with the peace marchers. I don't belong to any generation. My parents were too old and too young. They gave birth to the children of the thirties when they were in their forties and we've no generation at all. Oh, Leah and Peg are cool and separate, but Rosie's back in the nineties and look at me: I've got a bit of everything from 1919 on and what can I do with it? But don't let me saddle you with this personal mush. I'm going away."

"I'm afraid for you."

"Afraid I'll go to Ibiza and take lovers?"

"Is it Ibiza now?"

"Next year, Hydra."

"Don't, don't, be flippant, Sarah."

"I'm trying to wean myself from islands, and I'm very much a missionary about lovers."

All her bravery flashed out. "I think you'd better see a psychologist about that."

She couldn't say psychiatrist so I let her off, let her and Sarah Bastard off. "It's not as bad as you think," I said; "I'm very honest for a dishonest woman."

"But you do blame society."

"No. I name the name of history. The things I do as pitifully inevitable beside the product that I am."

"You don't take responsibility."

"I'm a psychological determinist. I should have stuck to Spenser and not had time for modern literature, but it was not in my character. I wish someone had bashed me and killed the Australian-Canadian idea."

"You are not a Spenserian by nature."

"That's what I mean."

I suppose I drank four brandies; because I heard myself crying and it was a cry, the kind you can't describe now because everything is self-conscious and cynical, sentimentality's away from us for another ten years; yet if I was sentimental, I was genuinely suffering from that excess of emotion. I said, "Why can't we like the old, romantic things any more? Tenderly, tenderly, day I have loved—My heart is like a singing bird... you see, I have to try to be of my own generation, but I'm stuck somewhere else, in sobs over Chu Chin Chow, how beautiful it was, my mother..."

We managed a quiet, formal parting, but I sat later and dazed on the steps of the subway and cried.

You see, alas, my mother...

Lyle perhaps sits there now, thinking, Sarah wanted me to be her mother. But she has a funnybone somewhere, I may have hit her, and I want to hit her now as hard as I wanted to strike out at my mother when I thought she knew me, when I thought she cared about me, the inside, personal, lonely me. God, I'm making Lyle into my mother, that's incest, my specialty. People are fools to accuse me of Gomorrah. And all the while I thought I had a straightforward Oedipus for papa.

Still, all the imagery for opening up a mind must be sexual, it's the same process. So all intellectual missionaries tend to lechery.

And Mother?

I tried to open her mind, too, don't we all: fifteen on a kitchen stool, proselytizing the minister's daughter of the nineties. This was considered an intelligent milieu, certainly most of them went to university, and that part of the world which it excluded couldn't be thought about. A nice girl, reasonable brain, and damn well not roving. But out of it. Her stories were of adolescent shyness, fear: fear of father, fear of public opinion (the Congregation was an ogre), shyness of her friends. Whenever anybody, even when I was ten, told me autobiography I identified, but I was never quite able to carry that fear for her. She was, then, a big and not gentle personality, fear having constructed hard edges; but a gentle mother; the opposite of my father, whose sternness was put on.

Mother was us, and underneath all she believed in—love, mercy, magic—she had a toughness and a fear. She had feared her father; the mother was distant, invalid. Perhaps the British are right to separate the child early from its mother, hoping to escape the seven generations' transfer of the consciousness of sin. But what shall we pass on if not what we are?

There went a pretty girl, my mother, and a nice girl, but strong. Once someone said, I met your mother, Sarah, she's such a lovely frail lady. Frail, I said, frail, and I, fully grown, thought, thank God I'm bigger than she is now.

She was our love and our hate, looming bigger than the Cheshire cat, and when the sun shone, more beneficent than God. Examining eyes like an owl's.

Now that I am at last grown up I weep to see her from the outside, frail and opaque. She was all poetry, magic, power, and strength. You could light candles to her and make incantations. Now we have all expiated her, like a sin. I wept for her and for me and for Lyle, and of course for Antonio on the steps of the subway, then went home.

I wasn't surprised to find Eldon, eating jelly babies.

You putrid old puzzler, I thought of saying, I'll give you ten bucks to finger your balls and prove I'm not out of the ordinary. Instead I said hello as if he were the cat.

He offered me ten bucks instead for an engraving I had bought in Paris for twelve thousand francs when the franc was five hundred to the dollar.

"Get out, you're a whore." I pronounced it hoo-er, like the boys at school.

"Sarah, I don't understand you," he groaned.

"You weren't meant to."

Until a certain age, hers or mine I never found out, I discussed, hashed, argued, with my mother; then she took to throwing her hands up, saying "I don't understand you." I am a simple person, that killed my love. When I first met Eldon during a staff coffee party, I thought as I think now: he thinks he thinks; but when the chips are down, he throws up his hands, declaring the unobvious past his, thus normal, comprehension. I may have avoided the wedding, but I had enough interest to go and see the kind of program he recorded for that day. I watched fascinated. Eldon on the idiot box, his jowled face cracking with one platitude while in the church he uttered another. Every day, in every way. Promising fidelity, he recommended reforms twenty years out of date; offering his sickness and his health, he discussed issues that in other cultures were buried and putrid. Offering to worship with his body, he recommended to us to preserve what was already gangrenous.

I sat composing a photograph of the Porlock sisters and their men, slipping Joe in for comfort: merchant, mountebank, student, prince. Drew no conclusions—except that the blood tie is overestimated.

This year we are big on Eldon, and since he is not entirely stupid, next year we shall be big on Eldon too. After that, as he knows, he will fade. But that is time enough, for a down-payment on a future. He's a good performer, in spite of his twaddle, and afterwards he will become Dean of Something.

Scorn not the fat man, Sophomore.

If he were right, if I could find in my heart to say honestly "but Eldon is right," my guilt at my scorn for him would go away, it could be turned against myself. But since his platitudes are taken seriously here, because I have striven to belong here, my relationship with *here* is made intolerably complex by Eldon, and I am forced, guiltily, to take him seriously. I must follow his outdated arguments about maximum security prisons; I must approve his efforts to persuade the country people of the value of even paint-by-number art. For assessments of this year and next year must include him, and eventually he will write a book and join my field.

I prefer to flee.

By Gomorrah, there was a suggestion that there be a sex course at St. A's, that Eldon, physiologist, give it. I coughed as if to puke. Well, they'd learn where the double standard stood in 1922, the thirty-nine-year-old centenarian.

Now Eldon Ombudsman is going to beg me not to leave the country. His bleached eyes on his jelly babies, he begins to speak of the "brain drain," of the evils of expatriatism. Of personal loss impinging on Principle. I see myself a subject of a fifteen-minute segment of "Professor to the People." His sister-in-law whom he was fond of, after all, the sister of his wife... a link not to be scorned—a fine mind... original research—a good teacher... one of the brightest products of our system... thousands spent on her education, thousands of public money... up and huffs off to Europe on the grounds that Canadian life isn't satisfying... who if not this kind of person is going to make Canadian life satisfying?

He ruminates and pleads: "Are you really going to go off and live among the dissolute expatriates on some damned island? They are dissolute, Sarah, they're wasters. They're wasting every valuable gift this country and God have given them. Drinking and smoking it away. Go on, laugh at me. Laugh at my old-fashioned values. But people like you—and Peg, and me—have an obligation. Not to bury our talents. And at a time like this when more people are going to university than ever before..."

"I'm not so sure of the value of that if people like me are teaching."

"Well, if you think you're a bad teacher spend

some of the time you waste drinking and running around and writing those God-awful plays becoming a better teacher. What's wrong with teaching, anyway?"

"I hate it, and I don't know my subject well enough."

"You're a silly, childish monster. You don't need London or Paris, you need a good, solid year of study here. Ask Lyle for a sabbatical to do some reading."

He's a deft devil, and I have to take him seriously. "I thought of that, too, you know."

"Well, why did you turn the idea down?"

"Because what I need is not a year's solitary with Ruskin, Browning, and the boys. I need two things— fresh air and some minds to sharpen mine on."

"There are hundreds of perfectly good minds here."

"Oddly enough there aren't. Something happens, Eldon, once people settle down here. The edges are dulled—news takes a long time to come, and ceases to seem important. It's something in the air, and perhaps a fundamental disbelief in temporal values. The only literary thing which really interests me is what is happening to literature now, why people write what. But we keep ourselves isolated from—the passion of making literature—from the passion of discovery. That's why we don't produce anything. And I want to produce, I want to get into a world where creation—creation of anything—is a fact, where ideas are important, where people are tough on you and where if you turn out something good nobody, but nobody, will say it's 'cute.' I suppose you think I could get some of this feeling from my friends in the academic but there's not a sharp edge on anyone who's taught more than a year. They're all too busy writing and broadcasting and providing for the second car, and that's that. I'd rely on Joe's journalistic friends, but in my line they're not well enough informed, so that's that. I'm going."

"Sarah, you're too much of a snob to know what's going on in your own field."

"Balls, Eldon. There are three good novelists in this country: one's French-Canadian; one's Barbadian; and one's Hugh MacLennan. All the others have been eaten, or live abroad. I'm not strong enough, maybe I don't have enough real personality of my own, to survive in a climate like this. And if I can't write, I want to do something more—more factual—than teach, something that doesn't allow me to fall back on personality, on acting. I can do translations, work with one of the press agencies, type—I'm no better at sitting all day on a bar stool than you are; I have to be really tired to enjoy an island."

He eyed me sourly for a moment. "Bitch!"

"Why? Because I tell the truth?"

"Because you've got no feeling of duty—toward the university, or toward this country."

"What did you do in the war?"

"Now don't start that..."

"Sorry. I didn't know it was a sore point."

"I was one of the ones who were turned down for the forces. I stayed in university and did war work at night."

"And had it held against you? This is a grudging society." But there was nothing to feel sympathetic about. Except perhaps that the keenest minds had been away, perhaps. I wanted to tell him about our war, about patriotism's being a war-saving stamp for a birthday present, and being made to march and sing those eye-stinging songs about Glorious Britain, and the Canadian ones which were set to American marching songs. About the proper use of propaganda in the direction of the young, about the gritty disappointment in the guts when we war children catch sight of the England there'll always be; then the insight into Australians and their "Pommies," and the glint in Father's eye as he hears us sing our propaganda and declares against the private school. But all this is too good for Eldon, I wanted to write it out again, and more, under the title "Jingoism is the Opiate of the People some of the Time." So I let Eldon take it from there.

"Has it occurred to you that your kind of rebellion is out of style?"

"I thought from what the paper said I was distressingly in."

"You're rushing off like some half-cocked teenager in the fifties. These are the years of staying home."

Why reply? He was answering my argument. Since I returned from Europe, I reckoned I had spent at least an evening a week explaining myself, and on this level, and often to Eldon. I was beginning to feel like someone in Feiffer. "Two hundred bucks," I countered.

He was shaken. He dropped his depleted bag of jelly babies. "What for?"

"The engraving."

"That?"

"It's worth it. Or you can have the Braun-Hogenburg Venice for two-fifty." This with confidence in his tightness.

"You picked that up in some flea market and framed it yourself."

"I love families, I love them. Because I'm related to you—only by marriage, thank God—everything I own has to be worthless and I'm not allowed in the better department stores. Speaks well of your opinion of yourself!"

"You are the most repulsive, dishonest woman..."

I shall miss Eldon. "Why don't you come with me? I could show you all the evils of Yurp."

"Thanks, I've been there."

"Keep your old Switzerland. Happy television."

"When are you leaving?"

"When I go."

"When is your lease up?"

"You forget that I live with the people and pay by the week."

"Well," he said, finally defeated, all his jelly babies gone. "Give us a call before you go."

"Love to old Peg."

"I wish you meant it."

"Oh, to her, yes."

"Good night, then."

XI

So exit Pinch-Me, the Tit-World Pimp, protector of God and Institutions, proclamator of the pre-eminence of Church, State, and Corporation. Protector of power.

Not a bad fate for a fat boy from a small town, the wielding of influence in the interest of Interests, especially if you believe in them, and most of us who grow up in small, scorned places do, it's only a flip of the coin whether, after *With Clive in India* you go on to *How to Win Friends and Influence People*, like Eldon, or *Be Glad You're Neurotic*, like me. If you're nothing, if your father isn't the doctor or the minister or the millowner, you know you're nothing, and what you weave out of that knowledge of nothing makes you burn twenty years later and, if you're in luck, you're sorry for the doctor's kids and the millowner's whelps, who have nothing to prove.

Eldon decides that God created institutions—from the country school on up—and links his life with their unequivocal respectability. All else is banditry, even those institutions subject to change with governmental power are suspect. And Art! The only painters he can bear hang from the breast of Mother Esso, his favorite writers carry out commissions from banks or teach in the larger universities. Broadcasting and the subsidized arts hang on the vagrant and fearsome fringe of Government. He does, as well, but regrets it. He won't be happy until there are only insurance companies, department stores, supermarkets, hospitals, funeral parlors, and IBM machines. Life will be tidy indeed, with Eldon crouched in a foetal position in the lap of the Greatest Private Entrepreneur of them all.

A dangerous man.

Meanwhile, he interprets the purple eminences of Toronto and Montreal; seated confidentially before their enlarged photographs, he points out their elegant steel-grey haircuts and their elegant aluminum collars. The grave gods of the status quo, just, righteous, and afraid of International Communism, liberals, and men from Abroad in badly cut suits, admired, admirable, pursuing their faulty interpretations of other people's lives, ready with their interests and their grants to save us from ourselves—they lean on Eldon's dewlaps for their images.

It is already a very nice world they operate, but it is the Tit-World and it can't catch me—without my knowing it.

More important, it doesn't catch anybody else of importance. Only the center-cut sirloin of the middle class. The norm is so narrow the rest of us fall off. It would be interesting to know what percentage of the population has to be out on a limb before the society disintegrates.

After Eldon left I indulged in pleasant thoughts of catching and labeling cockroaches for the pockets of DIRECTORS. As follows:

> *To the receiver: I am not a cute critter who operates a typewriter in New York. A mad Czech did not invent me. I exist. I carry Toronto on my back...*

Signed—Archie Roach? Wasn't that Cary Grant? Come off it, Sarah. Leach. You wanna be a cute kid with a beetle in a matchbox and get in Christopher Robin? Your nuisance value is nil. And the Tit-World gives with one hand a different freedom from the one it takes with the other. How easy it makes the insect forms of work!

I allow myself a moment of wistfulness for St. A's; its framework had saved me years of time, thought, and effort. Going on the Tit is like joining the Diners' Club, or hiring a maid: you don't have to carry everything on your own shoulders any longer.

Well, I was off. No doubt later I would panic and long to be on again; meanwhile, the thing to do was get over self-satisfaction. So I was off, and so what was I going to do?

I blew smoke rings for a while and pretended to think. Someone else who had never been on passed the window. God, I thought, it's slobbery to live here. For all my posing, I hate these people physically. You have to romanticize them or mow them down with machine guns.

Off the Tit, off Glenholme bloody Place. Will I

have the courage to face the auctioneer? To go? To stay off? And what to do with the recurrent vision of Sadie Porlock in a twin set teaching English in Peterbell, Ont.?

When I was religious I thought of this kind of vision as a gift from the Hound of Heaven, one of his nasty little Sunday afternoon tributes. I did not know then how evil it is to spend your life in discontent.

Desmond phoned, saving me. "How are you now, Sarah?"

"Surviving."

"That's as well. I was wondering, are you really leaving us?"

"Of course."

"And when would that be?"

"In a month, or a week."

He paused, evaluating my vagueness. "I was thinking of you in connection with something."

"Job in Dublin?"

"Horrors, if there was a job in Dublin, I and fifty thousand of my exiled countrymen would be flying after it."

"Loud chorus of 'Deep in the Canadian Woods We Met.'"

"That's it. So you're still thinking of the other side?"

"Definitely."

"You wouldn't do a job for us for the 1967 Centennial?"

The omnipresent Tit. "No, Desmond."

"Pity. I could get you seven hundred a month."

I had turned into a saint already. "No, Desmond."

"Well, would you like a little two-month kind of job to raise the money for a hairdo or a farewell party?"

"No, Desmond. Listen—give it to Joe."

"I'll think it over, dear."

I had shot all my intensity at Eldon. Now I thought, "Nice man, Desmond," and lay back again, generalizing about Irishmen, stage and real. Ireland might be the place to go, an antidote to one's unwarranted affection for the export version; Jas. Joyce in a top hat, Georgian terraces, Thomas L. Thomas crooning "Macushla"; that film about O'Casey without an Irish face in it. How well do I know the place, the literature? I pay lip service to a thousand things, fantasize without facts. I should go to all the places I have pretentious ideas about, kill the romantic in me.

Eliot speaks:

> *... human kind*
> *Cannot bear very much reality.*

And a professor I have never forgiven: "Women with intellectual pretensions always adore Eliot."

Wherever I go, I shall find myself looking for a pair of arms.

And there are places I have been already. That Greek island with Sandro: Cythera.

L'embarquement: from Brindisi on a day so steely in the sun that it had been flattened into a dock. All Brindisi deserves to be. The heel of the boot, squashed. I embarked alone and awkward, amid the seasick returning Greeks, the headstrong tourist pursuing an idea or a fashion.

The real Greek islands, the poster islands, are the Dodecanese, the Cyclades. Cythera is rough at first, raw. It took time to discover its corners. Then Sandro arrived, turned the place to trauma. After he left, I sat in my house for a whole day, stunned; unable to chase away enormous well-being with guilt. Simply *had*. The cliché—I was not to escape anything. Then the old woman who owned my house cackled in and spat on my face. I picked up my idyl and fled, not daring to wait until the disgrace sank in. A Greek on the boat recognized me—how we had been watched!—said they thought that Sandro was my brother. It was like Cacoyannis' *Zorba*. Now I should like to set out for the gentler Cyclades, and am afraid. Inevitably, sunk in memories, I would accept a pair of arms, but to be spat at once is enough, for there is no reply.

"Oh, he was not my brother!" I laughed, relieved.

"But he was not your husband. He was another woman's husband."

"I'm afraid so."

"You have no shame."

"I have great shame, but I do not want to feel it now."

"You will," he said, the Greek. "You will. Like a stone in your belly."

I thought, well I'm a puritan, I'm used to shame. But it was hard, and instead of my Antonio, still I carry a stone.

Yet if someone were to ask, as in one of those

question games, "What was the central event of your life?" I would not know what to reply. Sandro, the affair with him—and its end, because it ended, a month ago in New York, bitterly—will it not be on the periphery in ten years? Was it not more an effort to jerk my life out of a tendency than a personal act for its own sake—in other words a piece of opportunism? An attempt at a violation, the first hesitant step away from the Tit? Dutch courage, also, for there were better methods of breaking away.

There's no use sitting wondering if I loved him. I had such a passion for him that it wrung the identity out of my ears. I lost myself, I lost everything, for three years, but passion cannot be a permanent condition, and suddenly like an overwound watch, it stopped, and I found myself left with a few springs, and the things I had learned.

Now what do I need? Faith. Resolution. The virtues as outlined on the covers of exercise books: Be Ambitious, Brave, Cautious, Diligent, Excellent, Fair. Be these, and reconstruct my already Victorian life. Tonight the auctioneer is having a look at my furniture.

I want, I hear myself feeling, to lead an ordered and abstract life. I shall, and an empty one.

Smoke rings are whiffs of self-destruction. Freud died of them, and my father.

They say it's an optimistic end, *alors*.

Stop mewling around, Sarah, forget it. That's *the* answer, isn't it? Forget the corpulent past, move out, move on. You said you were going to, he said you were going to, *they* say you are going to. Turn in your life insurance like an old library book, sell the car to the brand-new dentist with the brand-new teeth who's been phoning and phoning—forget the whole lot. Live cleanly, live abstractly, stop mucking your life up with details, like the dentist. Why moan, mourn, or remember: why warm yourself with the faggots of gossipy asides? It's morbid, why that Marcel Proust he spoiled his whole life. Remembering is masturbating. Stick the past in the ground, keep your memories chill and stylized, start again, afresh, a-roving.

The auctioneer says, "Frankly I don't know quite what we could do with this lot."

"The pictures?"

"Ah yes, some of the engravings are rather fine. But you see, our clientele—if you want to make *money*—frankly I wouldn't. And the furniture... perhaps your friends?"

"The writing table is good."

"Ah yes, but you see, unless people, like yourself, have lived abroad, they don't want writing tables. Roll-top desks, yes—or pine—or, of course, office furniture."

I remind myself to stop having rude thoughts about people's teeth.

"Several people," I say feebly, "have admired the washstand."

"Well, you ought to try to sell it to them—or to the boutiques. You've got a lot of interesting stuff here—try the pieces individually in the boutiques and the antique shops. I'm afraid we just can't handle collections of tea caddies and lead soldiers, Dr. Porlock."

"Well, thanks."

Anyway, he did have flashy teeth and a horrible check overcoat and a mealy-mouthed accent. A long, self-important face. To hell with good resolutions.

Rosemary phones. "Sarah, you'll simply have to come up, Mother's very upset."

"I've sold the car, Rosie."

"Listen, I've told you I'd pay fifteen dollars for the table, haven't I?"

"I paid seventy-five and it was a bargain."

"But you've never polished it. Can Bob pick you up after the office? You and it?"

"He'll hate to, it will keep him late for dinner."

"Oh, he's working late, and then we're going out. You and Mother can babysit, Mark's on a date. Eat first, though."

"Well, I suppose so—but just me, not the table."

Submission. Then, in this processional day, a respite. I lie on this bed that I shall soon sell. A hard one, not old. Bought new on Queen Street three—no, two years ago, a "health" bed, you don't have to stick masonite under it for your back, that's what the base is. Hard to sell a bed, though. One of the second-hand furniture places will take it. God, worldly possessions, getting rid of them. Salvation Army has a double-garage-sized room full of dismantled cribs—who wants them? Get rid of it, give it away, go: a whole country's mentality.

And I don't want to part with any one stone I carry round my thick neck. Not a memory, not an arti-fact, not a book. In the back of my mind it is still evil to wear two coats, in reality I am stuffed with possessions. Citizen of the second richest country in the world. Look, my own car, rugs, bed, tables, sofa, dressers, lamps, bookcases, pictures, clothes, all this— things I consider necessities. So loaded I would like to give all to the poor, if I could find the poor. But every charitable outlet has a storage problem. People on this street inhabit furnished rooms, own nothing. More moral than me, except for knives, broken bottles, guns (yes, guns), razors, tongues. Should put up a sign, "Rummage Sale." Shall.

The books. Listen, these are my children, what shall I do? Try always to jettison anything I haven't opened for a year, but Jane Austen? All the Joyce Cary I wouldn't dream of rereading, but which comforts me? A fair section on esthetics. Canadiana? All first editions, here, mostly remaindered. What if I want to come back to teaching? How can I begin again? I don't read my books, much, I get my reading from the library, am scrupulous also about passing on paperbacks I have enjoyed; the books I keep are to warm myself beside: the same fire, for years. Since I was a kid I've loved the puce-colored Boston L.M. Montgomery set, Village Marty has offered a friend's price, but still?

Oh, I acquire possessions as a boat collects barnacles. Why worry? A year from now, somewhere, I'll warm my hands at another heap. Used to laugh at Joe, who collected stones everywhere—a piece of Versailles, the Louvre, the Parthenon, chip of windowsill from Cherche-Midi—and traveled heavier every year. Me, this little print, that teapot, two ashtrays, a mat, ring, shoe, clip, bookcase, letter opener, frame, basket, mask, lampshade, postcard, am I fat or only laden?

So every night I fall asleep reciting my rosary of possessions; so now. Hours before Bob comes.

Sleep, and into my sleep, familiar, pillaging Sandro. Pillaging, or pillaged. I feel him slapping against me, I pant myself awake, almost deliberately unwishing him, making myself celibate. A moment to recall Rosie whispering to Mother, "Poor Mark's had a wet dream." Poor? Better off than me. He's at the beginning? I put my head under the tap, full of the fustiness of an afternoon sleep, empty, dirty-mouthed, crumby about the eyes, and remember sharply. Not Sandro: Eldon, with his fat slapping.

So there we are.

Listen, Sarah, I'm sick and tired of you. Sick. All dreams and possessions and pretensions. Yes, pretensions. Pretending to be this woman and being that. Truth, stupid, truth, scream it at yourself, the truth lies somewhere in between. You've dreamed yourself into some sexpot, you've decided to live as a professor, you're not that, you're not this. Kill yourself, or decide. Babble about leaving a corrupt society, dreaming of running away. It's not this or that, it's nothing or both, learn to resolve, go crazy, or die.

Oh, Mother, Mother.

By the time Bob comes I have made myself neat, to eradicate the dream, which is still leaden as undigested flapjacks in my craw. So ice water, combs, clean shirts, and lipsticks are my weapons, it is a civilized Sarah at the door for him.

He's a poor weary fag-end of civilization himself tonight. His job's had the heart out of him years ago, but gladly, for the bank is his passion. Still, on a day like this you can see him wondering how he's going to divide himself. Six kids counting Mark, Rosie, now Mother. He makes money, mind you, but with the price of services and his banker's nature and his own decency, he's still the servant of his family, of his bank, his service clubs. There's no obligatory social life for him, he hasn't time. One of the grey-faced old-young; he negotiates investments day and night, and carries their worry. If you want a million for two days, go to Bob; he gives it to you for the bank, and sits down to worry.

We start to drive in silence. I watch his profile, strong and anonymous. "Bushed?" I ask.

"As usual, Sarah. It's a tough game."

"You love it though?"

"Some days. It's like any other job... sometimes good, sometimes not."

"Mother's so proud of you—she sees you as a power in the world of international finance."

"She's a nice woman." He says this carefully, in case I have been laughing at her.

But I have not. "She is," I say. And we go on in silence.

At the house, he disappears in silence again, until the buzz of the razor sounds. Mark clatters out, whistling. Two little ones are hauled from television to bed, someone is having a tantrum about a piano les-son, Mother calls "Just wait until I get Cathy out of the tub, Bob?" Another generation of clean ears keeps her busy. *Life* sneers at the English socialists.

The busy-ness of this household appals me. It is necessary, a condition for coping. Perhaps with Mother here it will be better. I remember her as mili-tant as Rosie, everything on the double, quick march, teeth, bath, bed, room for the next. Sheer hard work, this life. They claim to love it, and ask me in snide amusement what do I do, with all my time to myself?

Is this the answer? Up at seven, make breakfast, feed and clothe, send to school, cook, mend, clean, wash, feed, send to school, flop for fifteen minutes, go to a meeting if you can, shop, cook, wash, bathe, I should scream. I hope it's a life that creeps up on you gradually. I had a friend who cried out "They only keep you in the hospital five days now, it used to be two weeks. Why, the only time I get a holiday is when I have a baby." Five days in the hospital and two weeks' help after—a reason for a new life?

Ah, but when I'm called to kiss the polished faces of the new lives good night, and the hands reach up, and the smiles are on—there's more to it than that.

It is nine before they go out, and the youngest is awake for his last bottle. Mother with a baby in her lap, haloed by the lamp, welling out love, is a figure I had almost forgotten. The child is too heavy for her, but she will not part with him. Some of his weight is on the armchair, but he pants and pushes, gurgling his satisfaction. "The evening is the only time you have to enjoy your children," she says.

"He's a beauty, this one."

"Rosemary always has pretty babies."

"You look wonderful, with him, Mother." It is true, and her face is relaxed; older than when Dad died, but softer as well, the worry and the fear driven out by the job in her lap. I wondered what the least obvious feelings were when you were bereft of a husband after forty-one years, of a husband, of this husband, my father. Which of the myriad annoyances of cohabitation were spared her now? Which dependencies left her crippled? Nothing was showing, she practiced the self-control she had always preached, and, still, she must be mostly relieved by her release from the long hiatus of his dying. All of us by the time he died offered Death a guilty welcome. Now she is under the lamplight, holding a little boy.

"It's been a hard spring," she said. "A difficult time. Poor Dad. We're all looking better now it's over. Don't think I'm callous, but while he was in the hospital it was frightful. You were so good about visiting him, Sarah, and he appreciated it."

I appreciated the crumb of affection she was offering.

"We're all looking more rested, now." She stroked the boy's head, and nuzzled him and whispered to him. He had finished his bottle and was almost asleep. "I'm glad you're going on a trip, dear, you need it."

"I got the impression from Eldon that you were upset about it."

"I don't know why Eldon takes us so seriously. Perhaps, not having had any family... No, you do what you like, it's your own life, you're far too old to take us into consideration. I don't want you to be the unmarried daughter who has to look after her mother, I've seen so much of that, dear. I think we're all a little disappointed that you're leaving St. Ardath's, you scattered a little glory in our direction, but if that doesn't suit..."

"I'm not living the kind of life I want to."

"I don't want to nag, but I think you'd like to be married, wouldn't you?"

"I'm getting a little old for that."

"Don't be foolish, child. Girls of your age usually make wonderful marriages, you're old enough not to marry for the sake of it, you know what you want."

"I feel about ninety, I'll be glad to go away."

"I hope you'll see Leah." The first flash of anxiety.

"I imagine I will. Not right away. But she usually comes to Paris in the fall. I'll meet her there."

"She's the one I worry about."

"Funny, I thought it was me."

"No, you've always been contrary and rambunctious" (dear, family words), "but underneath it all you've got sense. Leah's what we used to call flighty. Is she getting on all right with her husband?"

A longing to confess convulsed me; I shut my teeth for a moment. "As well as—well—they would. You know them both."

"Not so well. No, Leah's not a sticker."

"He wouldn't let her go."

"What a strong man he is! And there's no divorce there, is there? All the better for her, I don't approve of people living together in hate, but some people need to be made to stick to things. Are the boys still sweet?"

"It's a long time since I've seen them, but I hear they're brilliant."

"I thought they were too—foreign-looking—at first, but in the latest pictures they look like two little angels, though of course their hair is turning dark. Sandro's face is rather coarse, they seem to have Leah's refinement."

The baby interrupted us with a sleepy squall. I carried him up, she changed him, we tucked him in his crib. I thought, he's so different from an imaginary child. He's self-contained; he has a self one never quite achieves for dream children.

On the way downstairs, "Dad was fond of Joe, you know, Sarah."

"Was he? He disapproved of the arrangement, I know that."

"Oh, so did I, but we were a little proud of you too, making him make something of himself after what happened to his wife. I used to think it was a pity you couldn't marry him..."

Lovely to talk to her again after so many years' pleasantries, feel her feeding me half-sentences, to return them. "No, I wouldn't marry him, it would be too much like never giving anything away, carrying all your own past on your back."

"You're a great one for house cleaning, aren't you?"

"Figuratively."

We made tea, and enjoyed the old argument, should you steep it in half a cup of water, or in the whole pot? She won, of course. And we were halfway through our party before we began to feel self-conscious again. She was tired, and there was no way for me to go home. She started to talk about the virtues of Bob and Rosemary, and stopped, waiting for me to criticize the bourgeois. It occurred to me to call a taxi, but I didn't want to go yet; it seemed that this was some kind of farewell, our last intimate evening before I went away.

"You shouldn't worry about Leah," I said, "she'll go on being herself. Sandro's hard on her, but he's generous. And one day she'll resign herself to life's not being an absolute dream of bliss. She's lonely, though."

"Does Sandro object to her making friends?"

"Sometimes. She chooses poorly, as if to annoy his family. But then, he's away so much."

She sighed. "We all have to learn to deal with our own lives. There's no hope otherwise." Instead of lives she might have said husbands.

"I think I'll call a cab."

"Oh, stay until they get back. It's so expensive. Or perhaps Mark... no, he ought to go straight to bed when be gets in. No, you stay and read. You won't mind if I go to bed early?"

"Of course not. But I am taking a taxi."

"You never liked to be cut off from home base, Sarah."

"And I guess I never will. I'll comb my hair, and phone."

On the way upstairs I glanced into the hall mirror. She saw me, and smiled. I had been much teased for my childhood narcissism and never lost the habit of the identity-confirming glance. "You're looking lovely these days," she said. "Suddenly your face has matured. The lines around your eyes give you character. Each of you has gone through a stage of being the prettiest, and it's your turn now."

I looked again, and found, to my astonishment, that the face was good. Not what I would call pretty, but, by heaven, an old master of a face: lined sufficiently to cut the roundness, shadowed under the hall light, the eyes deep and wide-set. It was the face I had longed for; it shocked me and blasted more rocks from my foundation; this face, had it always been with me? I had sneered at men who said they loved it; I had called it the face of an elderly pug. But these last months had refined it, lined it, thinned it. I stared at the face and thought "There's no excuse for me now."

Because with a pretty face and good legs you have to live on different presumptions.

Ours was a soft, affectionate parting. Tonight we had, in a way, completed our relationship. For a time we had hated each other; later and before, there was an element of fear. I had been for too many years dependent on her good opinion, had stayed too long adolescent, clinging to her affection; then disliked her because of this. Now, feelings had fallen in place: detachment had set in. She was preparing to be old, and I was preparing to be free. I left her with her second-generation family, and took my taxi down the Parkway in the black, warm rain.

When I was old and ugly I talked to taxi drivers, but tonight I had to practice reserve. I felt as if I were Leah. I simply asked him to stop on Bloor Street, got out, and began a zigzag walk through town.

It's an ugly town, a boring town, and they keep tearing the best parts down. They don't know what they have so before you leave you have to say good-bye to your favorite buildings: in ten years the mansions of the Annex will be mourned. I headed down Spadina exchanging the YMHA for the glorious *pigeonnier* of the Connaught Labs (and I had seen pigeons housed in cliffs in Greece, and tasted them) to the fake Etruscan firehall on Bellevue Avenue. Nothing to see, really; just a monument to someone's risible taste. The firehalls in Toronto are mythic in their splendor, and always sincere. Copies of nothing, utility and fancy adding up to epitome. Painted brick, heavy woodwork, Italianate Victorian towers, arching trees; gardens tended between alarms; a child's peppermint memory of the gleaming pole. Is the fireman still in the second-grade reader? Oh, they're tearing down the firehall on Howard Street, Bellevue will be gone soon enough; my great-grandfather helped build the loony bin on Queen Street: it will be razed, in time, as well. Precious little past we have, and that will go, that will go. So we have to go to Europe to chew over what we were, even Indians.

On Queen Street there's an undertaker with bentwood and frosted glass windows; the taxidermist on King, way down, has a front unchanged since the 1830s. But the new dirty bookstore has plate glass and chrome stands, and pamphlets on Lesbian flagellation.

Always, some bent slob follows you at night; there's no lingering by the truss store. Once in the winter when I was garbage-picking for Styrofoam for my bathroom ceiling, I came out of an alley victorious and bumped into Bob; he was wearing a Homburg and walking from the Royal York Hotel with two colleagues. We stared and pretended it was a mistake. The other two men laughed. "Beatniks!"

I've had good night walks in Toronto; for although during the day you are forced to build the city into something it isn't in order to endure it, at night what you want to see, towers, signs, crannies—these things are cast into relief, and stagily lit. Mews-alleys behind markets, downtown terrace housing built for the soldiers of Fort York, it's all there—waiting for the wrecker's ball—for me to croon over; after the right kind of day, I am intense, incandescent, I croon.

But tonight, treasures are meager. I catch myself hoping every passing car contains a friend. I want to rest, have no appetite for visual strain. I walk without hate, without anger—without, in fact, the gemlike bloody flame. Secure in the knowledge that everyone who has built an ugly thing will die the same death I die, but without living the same life. If the place walked into the lake on its billion cockroach feet, I would watch without a feeling or a smile.

At home, there is a letter from Sandro. I look from it to the mirror, and, finding that I have repossessed my old and homely face, turn out the light.

XII

The citizens of Euphoria live on peanut butter sand-
wiches, brandy, and capers. And capers grow on
Cythera, flowering long-stemmed and wrong-petaled
in the spring: wet eyes in Tennysonian crags. And the
citizens of Euphoria rise late and dream of islands,
have no hobbies, rather, practice being generally
manic or necessarily depressive; their bawdiness is
genteel and hygienic, in fact, literary. They spend time
choosing proper political views but take no action;
enjoy self-analysis, worship the greenhouse in Allan
Gardens and visit it on winter nights when scrofulous
reality is broken to reveal essentials in the snow. Their
motto is "Only One Basket for Eggs." They are the
new, or the perennial, Peter Pans.

And this is a day to begin with a beer rather than an
obligation, Sarah Bastard, founding member of
Euphoria. Today, last night you swore, today you would
phone selected citizens of Toronto to announce your
impending retreat; invite them to a revel, to an auction.
But when you woke names stuck in your craw, the sun
shone and you thought the people of Toronto should
take off their clothes and lunch on the sinus-filling
grass, and be delivered from your voice for a little while.

You slept with dreams again last night. Fortunately, they are forgotten; impressions of worms, however, endure, a sign that this morning's *Globe and Mail*, left between the doors by the tiny man at five, will provide you with fodder for indignation. Columnists' fume and sociologists' concern, proofreaders' insouciance, set against the beatings and screamings of the alleyway. Other people's anger is good with morning beer, before the onset of the knowledge that action will not take place. The right brand of Bastard has not appeared on the market. In Montreal, Quebec, *ça boume*. *Ça*, in fact, *biche*. Pride, intelligence and corruption have mated and produced not despair but revolution. But not here. Change is either a generation or a millennium away. The life expectancy of the Indian is thirty-one, the lap of privilege fattens, you are in it, girl, courage, and another ale.

Because the way to change is political, and politics are not your line. "I don't know how," you said to the organizer, "this country produces Conservatives when the textbooks are geared to producing Whigs." "Grits," he said, his teeth gleaming. "Subsidized by a Grit government." "Well, Liberals." "Fortunately for us, it seemed to have no effect." "The Anglicans and the Tories were the Bad Guys." "So you knew Chick Calhoun up in Sarbury? How's old Chick, have you heard? Used to be our organizer before he got laid out with his bad heart. Hello, Allan old man..."

Having in England sat on cold Trafalgar Square, I wonder about myself, if ten years could be shed, and now, and gasoline. This is what we youngsters think is politics.

Well, mail, then.

"Dear Sarah"—let me hold my breath.

"Dear Sarah, I have been thinking more and more about our meeting in New York"—you should, you ramping monster, you turned me into a small green turd—"and that I owe you an explanation"—you don't, you don't, remember your Waugh, never apologize, never explain—"and that I have now quite comfortably stopped loving you." Thank God. Love is a claim, Sandro, I don't want your claim, I'd rather make them. Me for the unrequited, it's guiltless, seamless, and fine. Go on.

"Sarah, when I met you I was one man, and now I am another. And although it is sad that our love has been lost in the change, it is so, for the legendary figures we have made of each other have come tumbling down. In New York, the sight of their ruin made us angry. You are the first woman whom for many years I have been able to take seriously, but I have taken you wrongly, as you took me. And the deceit and disgust of a long and expensive affair wore us out—something is now broken and gone.

"But not you, who have turned into my sister, I find.

"So let us begin to make ourselves clear."

I wish I were a woman who threw things. If I were—oh, if I were. Bash Sandro, bang life, lie still Antonio: I should have had my baby. I should have had the courage to tell Alessandro, his mother's precious Alessandro, long ago, "Finished. Enough." Manifestations of sibling rivalry, longings for security, these have been taken care of. Off with you. Then I shouldn't have to read him on paper, Sandro being a fool. Oh, he has insights. He sees that he has kept his empire small in order to hold his throne. "Like your Browning's del Sarto," he says, "I wish my reach exceeded my grasp. I wish I had tried to be other than an engineer and a businessman, an artist, or an architect. I wish, in truth, that I had tried and failed.

"Here, you come into my story, you and also your sister. When I met you both, I found a challenge; and both of you were, finally, in spite of your independence and your pride, easy, possible, and a disappointment. You made me angry, for seeming to be more remote than you are. A fault of my education, it may be."

Trolloping nuisance of a dead affair, a two-week assignation stretch into years of a banality that sickens fifteen-year-olds now. We fried ourselves in it, lowered and lessened us, lacerated old wounds. In his own context Sandro remains special, imperious as the sun, subtle as an adder. Reaching into mine, translating his feelings, he is a raging foreign fool chewing his own leash. Pretending Cinderella, I was Circe, reduced him, cuckolded my sister, and out of cowardice killed Antonio. Conventional morality does not enter—a tenth of the human population, an American Billion against an English, is fornicating against the rules. God save them, not making myths, legends, or monuments.

Repétez après-moi, mademoiselle (are you there, Gertrude?), a screw is a screw is a screw.

No furniture, I tell you, I want to live with no furniture, cut through the doilies to the center of the one-horsehair sofa, my eye on the main thing and no myths. So I surround myself with my Sandro, Joe, the idea of Antonio, a hundred pictures and pots, get rid of it all in a bloody flux every five years, and hear myself telling little female freshmen, "What did you expect, to sail through without mistakes? Looking for an eraser which will help you to the simple life? We used to call them rubbers, before we got sophisticated."

We Platonists may yet be wrong, and reality be facts, the superficial. Surrealists debunked. But scraping down to the facts is a lifework in an age of turgid prose. Or is the value of a book in its cover?

"When I met you, I realized that I had gone through my life without knowing another person, and I thought 'here is someone I can know.' I knew your background, after all, I knew Leah's stories of you. And I thought that the difference between you and Leah was that you were not beautiful, and needed to be loved; and that you were intelligent, and wanted an honest man.

"So I went to you and I was honest. I used my honesty to expose my feelings in a new way. I was as self-revealing as a boy of seventeen, and it worked like a magic charm. I think we were magnificently happy together.

"But all things change, people change each other, and when things changed I did not like it. What attracted me in you was your air of being mistress of yourself. Oh, now I know you were not. I know that the patronage of Joe was necessary to you; and when I very quickly (and you must watch for this another time, it makes you seem inconsistent and men will not trust you) obtained control of you, and you were my slave, I saw you grow smaller, and throw away your kingdom over yourself.

"At first I was merely sad; but there were years between our weekends, and I became angry, and then ashamed. I thought, this woman is one I thought was a queen, and she is only a liar and a cheat. She had the crown, but not the title, which I thought she had earned in chivalry, in launching-out. Or was born to. No, she was only an actress with a stolen crown. Am I the king that I once was?

"I began to understand a little look in Leah's eyes.

"All this took several years, and by the time I was able again to spend time happily with Leah, I was not so young. In fact, both of us have recently begun to acquire the characteristics of the middle-aged. In particular, we think before we speak, which is entirely different from the plotting of the young. Sometimes we look at each other wisely, and are tired, and I think, 'You showed me your sister in order to show me something about yourself.' And one day before I saw you in New York she said, 'Sarah still lives in a dream, and she does not yet know what she wants to be. Unless she marries she will stay a child.'

"You seemed no longer splendid. Had she taken the life from you again? I thought not. You seemed weak, unkempt, fat, and old. I struck you.

"Now I am sorry. But at the time I thought, if I reduce her I will start to grow again. My imagination had been possessed for years by something stunting, something that was untrue. I asked Leah, months—weeks, then—later, how I seemed to her. 'You've gone and got grey,' she said.

"So you two women are leaving me with just that. Grey hairs. I don't know what I have wanted, but it was not that. Forgive me for being angry, Sarah. I am a bit old, and life is not satisfactory. Perhaps my appetite is for something that does not exist. You were always attracted by hermits' caves, and rocks. Should I meditate in the desert? What women will I find then, in my illusions? This Leah who tells lies? This disappointing Sarah who lets go the strings of her life too willingly?

"I do not know. I think I have been cruel because of my ideas of women, which were not true. I think between you there is a truth. What I know is that now I am grey-haired, almost forty, and rather tired, my dear. I shall not see you soon again, but I enjoyed the battle almost until the end. When we are very old you will be kind enough to tell me what it meant."

Not the same guy on paper, few people are, he's mellower, when he hit me I saw murder, he's been drinking—what? One more who can't take it. I see myself as what women are, maybe he's right, it's a cross between Leah and me, where do you put the affairs? Damn him, damn Leah, damn me.

The life expectancy of the Canadian Indian is thirty-one. There's your reality, Sandro. Are we going to have to be Victorians all over again?

Well, *requiescat*, and with a wreath of caper flowers you-know-where.

XIII

Requiescat, also, St. Ardath's. Odd and honest for me no longer to wake knowing I have to face it, gown covering morning scruff, stumbling with sleepiness up the stairs to give, not get, the eight-thirty lecture. Every day getting worse, wondering if they were that stupid not to notice, or did the handsome, prosperous faces (how classes changed in ten years!) not expect more? At least they were tolerant, perhaps they felt I was honest, and easy to follow. I kept marveling at them, with their keenness, their memories. And I was never lampooned unless I chose to include myself in remarks against the "unwashed female academic." Not unwashed, dears, unkempt. I do all my reading in the bath.

I think my lectures this year have been largely confessional. Listen, I say, earnestness oozing, fact is I haven't remembered anything I read for five years. I get impressions—accurate impressions, generally—but the details are lost. I can tell you what to look for, how to go about learning, I can recognize untruth, but I can't recite the text. Take Ruskin—now Ruskin...

I have all the notes, the facts on boring little cards in front of me, I forget to look. Listen, I tell them frankly, I'm a substitute Ruskin-man, Ruskin isn't my line. But there's this you have to know about him, and this, and read Proust, and the new life of Proust which is... So they have Ruskin, Venice, the smell of the Zattere, Florian's, the Merceria, San Giorgio, James Morris's Venice, what could Proust have been doing? another Stone of Venice, the wooden bridge at the Academia, Millais and Millet, whosit's fecundity, Victorians who had child fixations, Pater's hypothetical accident, to what degree we are still Victorians, Ernest Jones in Toronto, *Sartor Resartus*, can you bear it, we ought to do some Carlyle, Jane Carlyle, letter writing, here's your reading list.

And I am thought not to be a frivolous woman. Why did Lyle believe in me? Sure, I got them reading, but that's high school stuff, they should have done all that years ago. Instead, in their first year (general course only) they listen to the side of Sarah that wanted to be a cheerleader doing locomotives for literature, riding hobbyhorses in exactly the manner of other academics she has scorned.

There was some thought when Linus Magder fell ill that I might teach American literature but this even the most cringing aspects of my character rejected. When I was a student the course included Emerson, *The Deerslayer*, Longfellow, and Poe. I wrote the exam on poetry we'd learned at home when we did the dishes (even Leah knows three books of *Hiawatha*), my reading here has been more eclectic (though also more thorough) than among the Victorians, and my prejudices are diseased. I should spend the entire year trying to insert *Under the Volcano* beside Nathanael West, preach against whimsy, accuse transcendentalists.

If this is a club, how the hell did I get in? They say I can teach, they say I know my field. Both these are only partially true. I can stand at a lectern and be my grandfather in the pulpit, bring to bear my passions and my aspirations for the congregation on the text. My field, a small one, is easy to know. But the material is so appallingly (to me) boring that I forget more easily every year what there is in it to know.

Who's to say I'm worse than some of the codgers who preached iambs at me? Lyle said my failing was spiritual pride, but I'm one of these humorless Canadians caught up in *should*. My only passions are syntax and prosody, others teach them better, *ergo...*

Ergo, books out of office, good-bye soiled grey plaster walls, false ivy (once identified in spitting rage by a mentor homesick for Cambridge), leaded windows, rotted grandfather's gown. Most of the books I shall leave or lend, the usual obligatory text. A few household gods I put up for show can go to Marty-the-bookman—battered Eliot first from Heinemann in Montreal, *Finnegans Wake* same expedition, the Canadian stuff goes to the library, bad as it is it's virtually complete, to *Sowing Seeds in Danny* by good old Nellie McClung. Send the Grove to Pacey? Burn that, I think. No, an earnest graduate student... Browning from home goes to Peg, she asked. Have I brown paper to send Ruskin to Leah? She reads odd hodgepodges, it's a good binding, still... Hopeful Sam Bosley is in the hall, he's the scavenger—perpetual graduate student, perpetual father, how else can he get books but hang around at the end of the year? Give him all the first year stuff, he looks lonely and sloping: I won-

der if anyone ever has made a pass, he has B.O.—stop
it Sarah, you're as fertile as trout, don't be feckless.

"You look damn glad you're leaving."

"I feel free. God, I was a lousy professor."

"Assistant."

"Well, anyhow, a fake."

"You had all the breaks."

"I didn't have a wife and five kids, Sam. How's it
going?"

"Any day I'm going to quit and teach high school."

"Why? Shoes?"

"She's been to every gynecologist in town, nothing
stops her."

"The Pill?"

"She forgets."

"Get her an I.U.D."

"I hear it puts you off for three months."

"So does a confinement, more or less."

"We manage."

"Get a mistress. Or do you want to go on?"

"I like kids, but I can't afford them."

"You have a nice soft voice and you love failure."

"Do I?"

"You could finish your thesis in three months and
you're dead scared of success. Or have you changed
the topic again?"

"Blaufeld wouldn't let me."

"He's no fool. You can have all my first year texts."

"I'd take your office, too."

"Sure you would. Your kids want the blowups of
Venice?"

"Jesus, you're really sweeping the past away."

"It's burying its dead, all right. Here, have you got the Cambridge History?"... Big-hearted Sarah sweeps thirty bucks' worth of new binding into his halitosis. Better soap and a toothbrush but who's talking?

"Do you think I could talk Dr. Lyle into letting me teach the Ruskin?"

"Not until you finish your thesis, you know the department rules."

"What'm I going to do? Shirley can't drive, the kids have to go to the beach..."

Shall I lecture? Shall I let him know? He loves his problems as I love mine. He leans on them. "Listen, Sam, years ago, well, three years ago when I first met you, the summer I was home, I worked out a nice five-point program for you. Let me know when you want your problems solved, Lyle has my address."

"The world's your oyster, isn't it?"

"My world is what I made it. There's not such a thing as luck, only opportunism, when you're talking about careers. But you aren't always going to be St. Ardath's poor boy."

"Take your fucking books..."

"Move your ass, Sam, move your ass."

My final academic profundity. I called Marty, we arranged that he would pick up the books. In the fusty, half-used women's common room I found brown paper, made parcels; phoned Eldon to meet—why not?—with him and Peg for lunch.

Well, new sister: pink and giggly. Eldon shifts from haunch to haunch and grins. They can hardly talk about their work, though word had it in the club this morning that Eldon was onto something genuinely, at last, scientific and Peg had a glorious contract with a museum in the States. No, she brushes it aside, she might not take it, it would mean being away. "Shall we tell her?"

"It's up to you, dear," Eldon dips and thunders.

"I'm pregnant," she barely squeaks. The only intimate thing she has ever said to me.

And she is pleased. She is bursting. She is, after all, thirty-five, married, childless. In addition, the ghost of tuberculosis has been swept away. "He said 'Let me do the worrying about that, don't let your mother mollycoddle you, and you should have a fine, healthy baby. Don't even go easy, yet. We'll see about that as time goes along.'"

"When?"

"The eighth of January. Doesn't it seem months and years away?"

"Eat your steak, dear."

Peg's little narrow face gathers into a *moue*. She should be wearing a cloche and doing the Charleston, she seems so young and happy and out-of-date. I have a smoky memory of her as a happy child, skipping rope before she went away. Bouncing Peg. "Oh, I'm so glad," I say. "So glad, and jealous."

"Sarah, we're going to have to marry you off."

"Eldon, we've been through this before."

"I know, but today I feel benign. Shall I order Chianti? Could you, Peg?"

"I've been living on Gelusil ever since I found out, but I hope I'm getting over the sick bit," she tells me.

"No, of course not, Eldon. But get it anyway, Sarah's going away." She has a new willingness to express her authority over him.

"Do you feel that you're normal at last?"

"No, it's not quite that. I'm more egocentric than you probably think. I've always taken myself as the norm—a defense mechanism—but I feel tremendously free and daring. I went to the San before the drug cures were very well developed and the TB-mystique was still very real. Imagine getting involved in it at nine! Even then it was pretty obvious that few of the young ones died, except the Eskimos."

"I know nothing about your case history."

"Oh, Dad felt very disgraced."

"Surely Mother..."

"No, she was inclined to take it as a kind of modern miracle. Apparently one of her sisters had just wasted away. She felt suitably awful, of course, but that was one of the odd things about Dad, whenever something went wrong he was inclined to blame it on a taint. Thought Leah's departure was like Auntie Millie running away at seventeen. I always had a sneaking feeling Mother thought it romantic..."

"She never said that to us. It was a big tragedy."

"Well I kept having terrible reactions to drugs and I didn't get my period until I was twenty-four."

"I never knew that!"

"That's the advantage of belonging to an old-fashioned family. Stop guffawing, Eldon, you're fascinated by women's talk, and you'll hear nothing but for the next twenty years, I intend to be house-proud."

He looked stricken, and she went on without

mercy. "I don't think they'll let me go through with the natural childbirth bit and since I'm overage and inclined to complications I'll have to do what they say, there's no use being headstrong when there's the child to think of, but he thinks just a local, and I'll see it being born and feed it myself if I can, and everything's been so normal, I've been as sick as your poor cat!"

She was bubbling over, but her steak was left untouched. She started to work on a plate of lettuce leaves. "People ask us a boy or a girl, but I think, oh, just a baby, and if that goes well, another soon after. Sarah, you can't imagine, I'm so changed, I keep going and staring at babies, and I took a really foul-paying job at Sick Kids just to be there. Oh, everything's changed."

"That's the first thing I've heard that makes me want to stay."

"Eldon wanted to tell you but only Mother and Rosie have known up till now. Many a slip... I thought perhaps Daddy, but she said no, he'd die worried."

Color in their faces. Beginning of a dynasty. You couldn't help liking them then. Becoming-parents feel threatened when people say "You'll change," but they all change. We single ones know we will lose them and we say, there are two less among the free. Not necessarily. People like Sam were born tied hand and foot, but among the secure and sententious, tolerance expands. "Party Tuesday," I said. "Come if you can."

XIV

I packed my trunk to go to China, and in it, I put—voices I had forgotten I had heard before; and voices I loved; and voices I hated, and voices that cracked and laughed and bawled.

"I wasn't going to come," the girl who was made of bones said. "I wasn't going to come, but I hadn't seen you to say I was sorry about your father, he was human and decent, and you were human about him. But I didn't see how I could speak to you because you've done nothing but betray me. Remember the friends we were? How we had Ideas, how we were going to make people listen? And you stopped. Even when you went traveling and I was jealous, although I kept saying, I'm traveling too, because my friend is traveling, and I'm traveling because I'm facing a world she hasn't the courage to meet, I'm home with Momma, but I'm beginning to live in the superconscious—even then I knew you were betraying us; all you did was flirt with the world, pretending to collect ideas, and then when you started to lecture, I thought—she'll do it; she'll be giving out the ideas *we* had. I thought you were big, Promethean, I wouldn't have cared if you'd betrayed me any other way, but you joined the poetasters, the 'fashionable young

Torontonians.' I couldn't speak. I hated turning out to be the strong one. I'm weak, and there's so much to do, so much to write. I thought maybe by teaching, Sarah, you could extend their framework, teach them the Way we worked out, but there hasn't been any indication. Oh, you're a madwoman, you've sold out the superconscious for love affairs and liquor, and the last five years the only sign you're alive has been lending me a book that convinced me I was a Lesbian which I, attachment to Mother notwithstanding, jolly well refuse to be. A madwoman's book, in the end she was reduced to rapaciousness, but I kept thinking, this is Sarah's book if she had the courage, she'd sell herself, it was as if you had written it, and it made me love you dreadfully, physically, and I thought, I don't understand *anything*, I've shut myself up for nothing. I have to say this in front of all these people, because you've made a well in my life, a well. You don't *know* the power you can be in other people's lives, just by being a strong—well, a strong-flavored—character. Well, I'm glad you're going. You're leaving me free. Ron and I are starting a press, I've talked Momma into it, the money. You'll have no part of it. You'll have to find your own way. And furthermore, I'm getting up my courage to ask Dr. Lyle if I can teach some of your courses. I've thought and thought, I know I have it in me, it's the right thing, to make amends for your lack of sincerity.

"You don't know what I'm talking about, do you? You lost me long ago. Well, I've gone farther than you, I've got a doctrine now, I know what matters! Words, the passion for words. Words as a way through to the truth. We were going to peel everything down to meaning, remember? Oh, we were kids then, you can look back and laugh, but I've never lost the importance of what we said, we were going to get through to the superconscious and I've begun to do it. You've got through to nonsense, you've forgotten anything else. It's all drink and love affairs with you.

"You haven't any talent? How do you know? Talent is keeping at it, ten, fifteen, fifty years on the same thing, just to get it right, and then crying it from the housetops. I agree with you about a lot of things, institutions, politics—but I let it pass through me, and get on with my poems. I don't waste my time on people, I work. But you're not listening, you're watching the door. I put a curse on you, Sarah, that shall give you such guilt..."

I went to take her in, remember, but a man gripped my shoulder, said, "Listen, a gripe against a society is a gripe against yourself; opting out is paranoid. Most places it's worse, and if you're not a citizen, you have no voice; you just become a café crank. I know, I've seen them: London, Paris, Ibiza—kids in cafés, swearing at Toronto. It's perfectly possible to live the life you want here, to be honest and scholarly *if* you're honest and scholarly to begin with. So I presume this is not the case and what you really want is to be another person. Not being able to booze on Sunday may be symbolic, but it is also unimportant."

"Dextri-Maltose," someone said, "may be laxative, but I find..."

"We've got them drinking, Sarah girl," sez Desmond.

And over there, voices: "And they had such a goddam simple marvelous life, every object had a specific value, and people used their lives, everything seemed to sing; they weren't hilariously happy, but they had satisfaction. They might have dreamed of affluence but they wouldn't have liked it, it would have turned them into paper-savers...

—Simple life, horseshit, they were politically irre-sponsible, ignorant, dependent on an authority that hadn't changed since the Middle Ages.
—Women are—
—Fascinating the way they are thinking of themselves now. As if they were feeling their new bodies.
—Cows. A woman on a delivery table, I know, before I specialized I did hundreds of confinements in the East End, women giving birth are cows, they grunt, groan, you won't be any different, you can't rise above it, not all the books you read and write as a sex will change it.
—How do you know what kind of person I am? What right have you to even try to find out? This is the sort of person I am. I'm a *man*. I shout, I hit you. Now stop trying to understand me; accept me. And get on with you."

"Peace," cries Desmond. "Peace be with you. You can stop drinking this here punch, it's too much for you who weren't raised on Powers, and cut into the beer. And Arthur here who's a diffident lad at the best has confessed his one real desire is to conduct an auc-tion, so we'll let him do it. Look, Sarah's bought good stuff, she's one of your rolling stones who can't help collecting moss, they're all the same, these girls who were raised on Eaton's Catalogue. Now she wants to get away, you can't blame her. Two weeks more at the sainted A's, saving your reverence Dear Doctor Lyle, and Sarah, being Sarah and not the intellectual all of us thought she was, but just a big girl with a lot of books under her belt, if she stays another week will grow a mustache and a beard. Now I know the argument's raging, about being an expatriate, but the point is, is there any place for single, gutsy women in Toronto? Now I'd like to say there was, and so would other people here. But we're all married and that's a fact. Now I don't want to send her off poor to become the concubine of some Turk, she has to have a little capital before she finds just the right pub to become the barmaid of, so before you fall down dead at the opening prices, remember, I was over two months ago and you can't buy your grannie's chamber pot in the Portobello Road, contents included, for less than fifteen quid, and while you were stashing it away to buy the down-payment she was knitting her own skirts out of dog's hair to go off to Turkey and It'ly and wherever she's been. So we're all poets together. Over to you, Arthur."

I didn't think I had such friends. But Marty had brought a collector from Rosedale, and, praise be, Des had a friend in the Museum interested in the odds and bits Sandro had helped me buy in Cythera, which were not Cycladic, but not young. Ruth had sent a note of obscenities, showing herself to be comfortably unable to live with those paintings shared by Joe and me. They went to a bawd—oh, such a bosom, such a face, she gives her husband a time—who was vaguely related to Rosemary's first husband. Braun-Hogenburg didn't fetch much, so I reserved, thinking to start again, but the washstand, the Mungo Martin mask, the Shiraz mat made money. And all the crap, you've no idea how they wanted it! So I've a two-buck Mouli and a salad basket from the Galeries Lafayette, a French four-storey porcelain coffeepot, a chipped Delft tile, a Victorian tile and a Styrofoam construction made by Joe — the hunger, the lust. The nestyness of my countrywomen exceeds the nestyness of me. Nobody wants the radio, but the framed Christmas card they must have. No obligations, mind you, no help-Sarah now: acquisition. Why didn't I open a Ye Olde Boutique, they're as bad as me? Tear the leaves out of the books one by one, frame, sell, gild the flower pots, stuff the toilet roll—now I see what men have against fat. The women are at it, bidding, boozy, cheerful. Faces sweating, consciences—how will we face the summer?—prickled, aware. This is how they live. Goods, chattels. Sarah's *mandoline*, not music, vegetable slices. Sarah's revolving bookcase, Byron, pass the brandy, I could sell my green stamps or my bum. Put your faith in fertility symbols—wooden spoons, clay bowls, trust in tiles. "Whatever you get from Sarah's authentic," Desmond says, and that's true. Authentic Kresge's plastic mixing bowls, grease-stained, fifty cents the lot. Four wooden spoons, one Swedish, one French, one Greek, one Dudley's Hardware, purchase value ninety-four cents—ninety-four cents.

Cheshire cat, me, swelling. One cat-bathroom,

contaminated: throw out, Arthur, for God's sake. And don't try to sell the underwear, try the cushions. Early Crippled Civilians, easily re-covered, whatsit, an apothecary jar, slightly cracked, real gold leaf and Latin, fifteen dollars to The Man...

He keeps a list, he's sober, and he's loving it. An evening of archetypes, everybody, especially husbands, having moments of truth. Murmurs of baby-sitters and one cries out "Shut up or I'll have a tantrum. I won't put on my coat. I'm at a party, so what if she's a bargain, let her rot, let them smother, I have a life, I was somebody years before I met our kids, they're full of crap."

"Piss on sconces," Richard Morley says, and buys Ruth's physical-therapy lamp.

The girl made of bones, the poetess, now miserable, rolls her calf's eyes. She's drunk on water, rubs herself against me. "Sarah, don't go."

"Shush, I'm listening."

"It's obscene, all your things."

"Objects are objects."

"You had that ashtray in your room at St. A's."

"The one whole term I lived in. Wonder why it never broke. Buy it and stroke it later."

"You are cruel."

"Didn't you know?"

"How can you part with things?"

"It's house cleaning. I'm domestic."

"You're disgusting."

This from another mouth, whose I don't care. So I'm disgusting. So are you and you and you and you if you choose to see it. Anus and vagina and penis have moved closer together as we stand longer. Unless we accommodate our smells and our necessities and our procreation, we go mad. Accuse the Jews of castration for circumcision: verbally incapable, the lot of us. And now we have sex and possessions instead of ideas, spit on Victorians, who had ideas, possessions, and the Lower Classes, who have, indeed, not died, next door there may well be a murder under cover of our noises: more likely something less sensational, a humiliation, desertion, a carving, a rape. Meanwhile, we spew our attachments.

This I love, this is good. If I could stay, and see these things always, I would. My friend the poetess is burning. Peg is not doing so badly, nor I myself. Worth Sandro. Worth Joe.

They're drifting, now. I'm a skeleton, there's only the bed and the sheets—all for Mother, who needs a second start. Stripped, I am. Right down to moving day.

Satisfied.

And friends are sometimes impetuous. Arthur and Desmond poured me onto the morning train to Montreal. I remember protests from Desmond's wife, who packed. "Never you mind," he said, "Sarah's going to have the time of her life." I sat pointing to things, a rich popular lady preparing for safari, and the men made labels. Mother. Peg. Rosie. Storage. They put my keys and a month's rent in an envelope for the caretaker. Arthur set aside a couple of ornaments for Joe. "Well, you won't need that," they kept saying, and they threw out the worst and the best of my past, and it was all on their shoulders. "The kitchen cupboards," I moaned, and Maura echoed. No luck. They were having the time of their lives. And me tobogganing to oblivion.

There was a lot of cash money, hundreds of dollars, everyone must have been as drunk as I. I slipped Maura some for the kids and made her keep it. Desmond bought me a bottle of 222's and bribed the porter to look after me. "Listen, Sarah darling, just lend me a twenty for the baby-sitter."

Whole bloody day it takes to get to Montreal and this time of year the landscape is hideously green. The green of careful lady painters in the twenties, screaming. No subtlety. Miles of paddy shot with crass yellow sunlight. Unreal. One day of the year it has to be that green, and the ditches full of mustard, and dandelions—water-color-box stuff. I thought, the sun will go in.

The sun wouldn't go in and the lake sparkled. When I wanted to keep my gloom, the last shred of yesterday, sailboats came out among islands. A creek of asbestos slag would have saved me but it passed in favor of ball parks looking rapturous and suburbs soothing. Jolts, stops. Unpainted stations that slipped by our Gracious Queen. Everything looking precious, components of a dreamland.

And I kept remembering how roads sloped off to the lake on one side, the highlands on the other. Thousand Islands and the cottages which were mansions of American millionaires. Rocks, shield, sheep, the other way: Milton country the skiers and the speedboats haven't begun on. Rambling hotels, abandoned homesteads, stone walls: native lyricism, Oh Susannah. And I remembered going to Sarbury one Christmas on a gaslit train and an old man playing "Oh Susannah" on the mouth organ by the stove. In fact, the native lyricism was beginning on me again.

You've got to remember back in those hills are some of the dumbest, narrowest people in the world, and they think they're better than Africans. You've been seduced by landscape before, kid, and wound up talking to trees. It's a long winter back in there, as it's a long grueling summer in Greece. The happy natives would be glad of a stranger to play with, but how long could you take it, three weeks? You're a city girl now, you need the *New Statesman* and *The New York Times*. Dandelions hurt your eyes and the women don't drink their poteen, they're busy having babies, scrubbing, peeling; count your lucky stars.

And these fine Loyalist towns along the way? Out of frying pan, in spite of architecture, into fire. Always misled by visual pleasures, aren't you, buy anything painted white. Not that there's wickedness in the cupolas or incest behind gingerbread, no—funeral parlors, Lions' Club, W.I., W.A., W.M.S., W.C.T.U., C.G.I.T., A.A., O.P.P., TocH and Chi Rho, or as we say it, XP, St. Andrew's, St. George's, St. Paul's, Central, First, Water Street, and the Holy Rollers. The King George, the Canton, the Crystal Grill, and the Maple Leaf. Library, Post Office, City Hall, Oddfellows, Masons, Knights of Columbus, and five schools. One's Scotch, another English. One respected citizen drinks, another still skulks behind marriage to his deceased wife's sister. Marvelous yarns, let someone else collect them. You've been here before, remember? Grew up in five of them, all farther west, population ten to fifty thousand, never any adjustment problems, except in the naming of marbles and the order of rhymes for ball. Time and immigration have changed them, but you know where, there, you would belong, and you don't want that—do you?

Should have married, should have gone insane, never strong enough to stay away from Mother's arms—landscape, white and red towns, schoolhouses move me, and not to say "how cute." Men see this, use me to feel good about, the way I use them. Cook for Joe, make Sarah temporarily secure. Still being torn?

I got out, didn't I? Train screams, I thought they didn't any more, in the west they sound like lake boats in the spring. More nostalgia, and with this head. To be used and useful.

Three days in Montreal, in the old Queen's Hotel, one of Joe's snobberies, parallel to my old women, arranged by him. I called a doctor who wasn't amused but administered a shot and a pill: some intestinal trauma, I said, on seeing the countryside in June. And Montreal.

Alone in it, and warming my five wits. Temptations to telephone all resisted, I wait until I become what I am.

Last night I started to walk this town. It's not the place I know from McGill-Toronto weekends or English-Canadian romance. Westmount, the Square Mile, and N.D.G. are ludicrous islands, they feel it now, and swarming and hissing around them are the people who consider themselves indigenous and indignant. The once-Beat cafés are full of writers for *Parti Pris*. Something of the Beat has gone into the Separatist movement, it's alive, man, alive, there's jazz-talk and glory among the bombs. For audience the rest of the country cocking its snoot saying "Who's bilingual, what do they want, we beat them and we're Ukrainian." College classique and lycée trained, these sprung young men write out their impassioned logic, laugh, incite the bombings. For this, and the despair of gasoline torchmen, I am too old, too old. But in the country of the zombie the rebel lives.

And Jesus, in another mood I'd walk right into the center of the thing and say "I'm Sarah, can I be your housemother?"

The crones are calling "Jesus saves, Jesus saves." *Time* asks what philosophy can do for you. Theologians cling to the fragment, afraid of plunging into the beautiful whole of the world-cycle. Physicians atomize the orgasm. With my nine hundred bucks I could feed a thousand African orphans, or go anywhere on a tramp ship in the world.

But tonight I'm in Joe's old Queen's Hotel. I'm looking out of the window. It's a new town. It strikes me, I haven't lived here. I hear them saying "She never got any farther than Montreal," I twitch with amusement, admit embarrassment, stick another pin in the shipping list: Lagos. I'm one person Africa doesn't need, and do I need Africa? No.

You know, what takes the real guts is not to go away, but to start again. Scarlett O'Hara cutting down curtains has nothing on me. There's that bar advertising "Sterilized Glasses," could I start there, shut my mouth, shift, learn, not fall back on bank accounts? Is it phony? Not as bad as a Separatist's housemother, not like a white cannibal woman in Africa. Listen Sarah, you've got no one to fall back on in this whole town, Janine's in France, the McGill crowd you've lost touch with, you won't meet your aunts in Eaton's, it's a whole new world. Back in Paris, you'll feel middle-aged and sad. In Italy you'll get a crick in your neck looking toward the inescapable Venetian light. Here you're nobody. There's nobody who's nobody like a lowborn Ontarian in Montreal. And so if you're a desperate old maid? No fear of being a Somerset Maugham one, choosing between radio operators and beauteous Polynesians, being literary, fighting.

It doesn't matter what lifts you over the hurdle. What creates the hurdle is a problem in sociology. But if you see it there, and you can put a name to it—

drink, drugs, incantations, bombs, petrol, Milton, solitaire, Tibetan prayer machines, these are legitimate means.

Jump, or you'll die, Sarah. And there'll never be green landscape or a sweet face again.

Afterword

To write this, I, like you, begin with the book. I retrieve an old dusty hard cover of *No Clouds of Glory* off my bookshelf. *Sarah Bastard's Notebook* was originally published under the title *No Glory Clouds*. It's been a long time since I've opened these pages. Reading the work of my mother has never been easy. Memories flood back and I am always left feeling very close and yet so far from her. It's this feeling of longing that keeps me away.

The copy is dedicated to my grandparents and reads: "To Jack and Lollie, love Pass." Pass is short for Passmore, my mother's maiden name and subsequent nickname.

A yellowed newspaper clipping falls out, no doubt collected from the *St. Catharine's Standard* by my mother's in-laws, Jack and Lollie Engel. It reads: "Women Writers are on a Literary Cloud of Glory," by Barry Campau. Marian is quoted: "Reading my book now that it's between covers is like hearing my voice on tape. It doesn't sound like me at all."

It's a long way off from Aix en Provence, Paris, London and Cyprus. Like her heroine, Sarah Porlock, Marian spent many years abroad, searching for her own path in life. Unlike Sarah, she did choose family life and marriage, but her career as a writer was never far off. She was determined to be a writer from the tender age of four.

The reviews of "No Clouds of Glory" in 1968 are mixed. The *Toronto Daily Star* writes: "Engel's cool, wry detachment to life brings a fresh astringency to the Canadian novel." Nora Sayre comments: "Marian Engel's talent is copious; her novel is clever, clear and valid... But Engel's heroine hasn't graduated past sarcasm..."

Sarah Porlock's messy life is full of contradictions, gross insecurities and hypocrisy. She is not a forgettable character and to some, un-likeable and unsympathetic. She is so human that I find myself thinking what a mess I am. Has my mother passed down the Sarah Porlock gene to me? Of course not, it's just the effect this character has on you. She is vividly human.

In *Sarah Bastard's Notebook*, Sarah becomes a vehicle for voicing my mother's frustrations with Toronto's mediocrity, small mindedness and smugness. Sarah desires beauty, inspiration and love but cannot overcome her own insecurities. She is her worst enemy and a self-hating tornado that tries to obliterate everything in her path.

Returning from Europe in 1963, Marian feels caught in a time of profound transition. Canada is changing but still has a long way to go. Marian is not afraid to push buttons and social mores, anything to move things a little further along. She openly discusses a woman's desire to choose her own path, away from the societal norms. She writes in her cahier: "I am riding my character like a horse these days – disobeying orders – living instinctively instead of logically. But riding high. I've bashed a great hole in the year – through to the destructive reality of the other side. The brass band plays of "God in the Gardens." The Victorian glasshouse."

Marian is also defensive. She wants acclaim and glory but longs for acceptance. She remarks on a comment made by Hugh MacLennan in her cahier: "Men will give me hell, he said, because I have talent. They will want mothering I can't give – and I will want fathering they can't give. I am to suffer & struggle & win."

She speaks loudly through her writing and becomes active in the burgeoning Canadian writing community. She goes on to become one of the founding members of the Writers' Union of Canada, and is an active member of the Toronto Library Board and fights passionately for the pro-choice side. She goes on to win the Governor General's award in 1976 for her acclaimed novel *Bear* and is made an Officer of the Order of Canada in 1984.

Marian says in a 1968 interview: "This is a great period for women writers, we're the second generation of educated women and we're having experiences and problems that have never been exploited before".

Interviewed at her home on Clarence Square in 1968, the interviewer remarks on Marian's Victorian home and her antique furniture. A bright yellow abstract painting sits above on the wall. "I bought it with my advance" says Engel proudly.

The painting is in my living room now and remains as a testament to Marian's dedication and drive to plod on into the unknown... despite the obstacles, bad reviews and coffee stains. Like most women, today I still face many of the same problems, but I know there are people like my mother who have made the road a lot easier to go down. Bumps and all.

Charlotte Engel
January 2006